Love is
a time of enchantment:
in it all days are fair and all fields
green. Youth is blest by it,
old age made benign: the eyes of love see
roses blooming in December,
and sunshine through rain. Verily
is the time of true-love
a time of enchantment—and
Oh! how eager is woman
to be bewitched!

THE SONG OF THE PINES

Taken to a Greek island as substitute for David Nicholas's secretary, Annie Frayne quickly falls prey to the island's charms, and to the charms of both Marcus, the Greek, and David himself. Her newly-born romantic longings involve Annie in an experience that changes her from a naive girl into an aware woman. For in discovering the reason for the love/ hate relationship between Marcus and David, Annie learns many lessons regarding life and other people.

CHRISTINA GREEN

THE SONG OF THE PINES

Complete and Unabridged

ULVERSCROFT
Leicester

First published in Great Britain in 1986 by
Robert Hale Ltd.,
London

First Large Print Edition
published December 1990
by arrangement with
Robert Hale Ltd.,
London

British Library CIP Data

Green, Christina
The song of the pines.—Large print ed.—
Ulverscroft large print series: romance
I. Title
823'.914

ISBN 0-7089-2329-1

Published by
F. A. Thorpe (Publishing) Ltd.
Anstey, Leicestershire
Set by Rowland Phototypesetting Ltd.
Bury St. Edmunds, Suffolk
Printed and bound in Great Britain by
T. J. Press (Padstow) Ltd., Padstow, Cornwall

1

ANNIE Frayne had never been abroad before. As the busy airport engulfed her, she stayed close to her boss's broad back, jostled by other travellers, hoping he wouldn't go too fast and lose her.

It was on the tip of her tongue to shout after him—*hi, wait for me!*—but the one look she had taken at David Nicholas's frowning face as she got out of the taxi five minutes ago to find him waiting impatiently, had been enough. No, little Annie Frayne, junior from the accounts department of the London branch of Incorporated Holiday Villa Estates, definitely didn't have the nerve to tell the Big Boss's only son to hang on and wait . . .

As the business of weighing luggage and checking tickets proceeded, Annie saw David's undeniably handsome face suddenly resolve into quick anger. He argued briefly with the girl behind the counter and then strode off; with a curt nod aside to Annie to "come over here". Standing his bag by an empty seat he glowered down at her.

"Someone's made a mistake over the flight time. *Damnation!*"

Annie said timidly, "Have we got to wait very long?"

His steely grey eyes didn't bother to look at her, merely flicked over her head, which reached just to his shoulder. "Half an hour."

"Oh well, that's not too bad—is it?" She wilted as the icy chips reluctantly moved her way.

"Bad enough. Sit down while I buy a paper."

Minutes later he returned, to plump himself down at her side. Annie, watching the milling travellers who filled the large departure lounge, was quite happily absorbed. When he suddenly growled accusingly, "Why didn't you tell me the flight time was wrong?" she nearly jumped out of her skin.

"Tell you? But I didn't know—"

"Well, you should have done. Surely you look at a ticket before you go on a journey, don't you?"

It was in her mind to retaliate by asking why he hadn't noticed the mistake himself, but with an immense effort she smiled placatingly and murmured, "I'm sorry, Mr. Nicholas." Then she glanced at the clock nearby. "Only another ten minutes now."

"Hmph!" The snort revealed just what he thought of such an inane remark and so she shrank back into her shell, thankfully following him to the plane when their flight was eventually called.

Before she knew it they were boarding the silver monster, her bag was stowed on the overhead rack and a seatbelt clicked around her diminutive waist.

"Sit still, we're just taking off." David still sounded irritated, so much so that her heart sank and she began to wish she hadn't been ordered to come with him on this trip . . . oh, to be back in the cosy accounts department now, having a cup of coffee and sharing a few words of gossip with Sandra before the work of the day began.

Sandra, her close friend, had been wide-eyed when she heard about Annie's promotion. "You lucky thing! Going to a

Greek island with David Nicholas! What on earth have *you* done to deserve such a break, I'd like to know?"

Annie had considered the question very deeply—it was a difficult one to answer. "I think he only chose me because his own secretary, Jill Martineau, is in hospital having her appendix out, and because . . ." Natural humility forbade her to give the obvious reason, but Sandra was a true friend and finished the sentence for her without any sign of resentment.

". . . because you're such a whizz-kid with figures and you can help him sort out the mess the Greek manager's got into. Well, all I can say is that it's been nice to know you for the last six months, obviously you'll never be a mere junior again . . ."

Annie had smiled back at her friend's wide grin and answered gently, "Don't be daft. I'll be home again in a couple of weeks, Mr. Nicholas said, and by then Jill will be back and he'll forget all about me, and you and I will go on sitting opposite each other in this grotty little room, with Eric beside us."

Eric the calculator made a strange whirring noise at that precise moment, and so the conversation ended. But Annie was to remember those last words with some wistfulness in the days to come.

Now all she could think about was the terrifying nothingness between her and Mother Earth, so far beneath. The plane had taken off with a whoosh that almost left her stomach behind and made her ears pop; she put her hands to her head, shutting her eyes grimly, until a bored voice beside her said, "You can come out now, we're up. Take off your seatbelt."

She fumbled inadequately. "I can't—I mean, I don't know how . . . oh dear, I'm sorry . . ."

"Let me do it." David's lean face was only inches away from hers as he unclicked the belt in one powerful movement. She slid a covert glance at him as he relaxed back into his seat. He was suntanned because he'd only just come back from a trip to the Holiday Villa Estate in the Bahamas and elegantly dressed in a light grey suit with a darker toning shirt that exactly matched his eyes; yes, David Nicholas was certainly a dish. He was also, according to office gossip, selfish, ambitious, spoiled, with more forgotten loves behind him than cups of coffee in the Rest Room vending machine.

Annie, suddenly very conscious of her rather insignificant navy denim suit and sea-green tee-shirt, wondered yet again exactly what she was doing here in the company of such a dazzling man.

She thought back to the amazing moment last week, when the phone on her desk had rung and his deep, smooth voice said commandingly, "Miss Frayne, I want to see you. Right away."

Eyes like saucers, she had risen as if hypnotised, mumbling something quite incomprehensible to Sandra and gone along to the big executive suite at the top of the building, with her mind in chaos. Had she added too many noughts to a cheque? Was she about to be sacked? Her timid knock at the door was answered with an abrupt *come* and in she went.

"Miss—er—Frayne, I understand you're competent at your job, even though you have only been here for just under six months."

A slight niggle surfaced with Annie. He sounded for all the world like her late headmistress, faced with a childish prank. Who did he think he was, for heaven's sake? The answer came with crystal clarity: *the Big Boss's son—so don't answer him back.*

Biting her lip, she had merely nodded, speechless, while feasting her romantic eyes on the handsome picture he made, the sun-bleached, fair-headed, good-looking man in the dark business suit, lolling in an expensive leather chair, staring at her with astute, hard grey-green eyes.

"I need someone to come to Doloffinos with me next week. Miss Martineau is in hospital, so it looks as if I shall have to make do with you. We shall be away for at least a couple of weeks, maybe more. Marcus Kalamares, the manager of the estate on the island, is having domestic problems and from all accounts the place is in chaos. I shall reorganise things while you sort out the accounts. Is that clear?"

His unsmiling, tanned face appeared very bored and very cross. Annie swallowed and put a hand on the back of the chair in which she hadn't been invited to sit. "Er—yes, of course, Mr. Nicholas.

Er—will it be very hot—I mean, hotter than England?"

"Of course it'll be hotter!" Clearly, he thought her an arrant fool.

Annie hurried to explain what was on her mind. "Then I'll have to buy a few things—cotton things . . . I mean, I don't have, well, you know . . ."

"I do *not* know. What are you trying to say, for heaven's sake?"

This was the point at which the scales fell from Annie's eyes and she realised she could quite easily hate him. Removing the timid look from her face she said pointedly and with spirit, "That I should like some salary in advance, if you please. After all, if we're travelling together, I don't want to disgrace you by appearing in my tatty old jeans, do I?"

If he had been hit by lightning, David Nicholas couldn't have looked more surprised. Annie had the feeling that people just didn't ever talk to him like that. As a result his face grew even grimmer.

"I see. Yes, that'll be in order. Draw a cheque for yourself and make it out to expenses. Will a hundred pounds be enough?"

Annie's face flamed indignantly. "I'm not asking for a handout, thanks, I'm not quite as poor as that! I'll just take two month's salary in advance if I may—that'll do me nicely."

They glared at each other. Then irritably, he swung around in his chair to gaze out of the window at the view of Hyde Park far below. "Right. My father's secretary will make the travel arrangements—she'll send your ticket down to you. Be at the airport thirty minutes before the time of the flight and I'll meet you there. Thank you, Miss Frayne."

Dismissed, Annie seethed momentarily but kept her head. "Thank *you*, Mr. Nicholas," she said coldly and marched out of the room.

His words echoed in her mind as she returned to Accounts. *I shall have to make do with you.* What a nerve! *Make do?* Annie swore there and then that she'd show him she was light years ahead of sophisticated Jill Martineau and her sweeping eyelashes when it came to figures. Oh yes, arrogant David Nicholas would learn a thing or two before the trip was over!

Now the plane droned on interminably. Puffy white clouds drifted past the tiny window at Annie's side and she began to feel sleepy. The last few days had been hectic, what with bringing her work up to date, saying goodbye to her family and buying one or two sun-dresses in her rushed lunch hours. Just as she was floating off into a delicious doze, the familiar deep voice rumbled in her ear.

"You'd better read this." A hefty file fell into her lap as she reluctantly opened her eyes.

"What is it?"

"The last six months' accounts of the estate on Doloffinos; you can assimilate them while we're here—save time the other end."

Annie's instinctively sharp rejoinder was silenced by the timely appearance of a beautiful air hostess, who smiled persuasively into David Nicholas's appreciative eyes. "Can I get you a drink, sir?" she cooed, and Annie watched his face relax; all the tension and irritation faded as he smiled back, letting his glance run up and down the girl's spectacular figure.

"That would be very nice of you," he said graciously. "A gin and tonic, please —plenty of ice."

"Certainly, sir. And something for the lady?"

Feeling herself forgotten, Annie sat up expectantly. David turned to her absentmindedly. "What would you like, Miss Frayne? A Coke or something?"

She nearly choked. Did she look such a child, she wondered, full of murderous thoughts? just because her chestnut hair swung loose and she was tiny and people often said how young she appeared . . .

"An—an orange juice, please." Immediately, she wished she'd had the courage to ask for a double vodka, but knew herself well enough to realise that, had she done so, the wretched report sitting in her lap would never get read.

Perhaps the drink soothed him. Annie, in the middle of her orange juice, was abruptly aware that he was looking at her in a new, more friendly, way. She thought him heart-shatteringly handsome, and when he spoke the note of wry humour made her blink.

"Miss Frayne . . . look, I can't keep calling you that, for heaven's sake. What's your Christian name?"

She swallowed. "Annie, Mr. Nicholas."

"*Annie?*" The grey-green eyes frowned. "Don't be absurd, you can't possibly be called Annie . . . it sounds like a kitchen-maid in an Edwardian drama . . . you mean Anne, don't you?"

"No, I don't." She stiffened. How dare he patronise her? "I was christened Annie because there are other Annes in my family."

"Really? How many?" He sounded as if she had confessed to having two heads.

"Three, actually. My mother's called Annette, my elder sister is Anne-Marie and my aunt is Ann. Without an e."

"I see. Well, as your aunt is unlikely to be in Doloffinos at this particular moment, I shall call you Anne. With an e."

"Then I'm afraid I shan't answer. I've told you, my given name is *Annie.*" She knew her colour had risen. Holding her breath, she stared boldly back into the terrifying grey-steel eyes. After a moment,

12

while she waited for an explosion, the icy chips suddenly thawed and grudgingly smiled at her. Annie gasped in relief.

"You win. My, but you're fierce for your size, aren't you, Annie?"

"I—I—"

The smile he flashed at her was overwhelming and she spent the next half-hour silently recovering from it.

And so the flight continued. It was three-and-a-half hours to the minute when the pilot's nonchalant voice informed them that they were about to land at Athens Airport, and Annie's mind abruptly went off at a tangent.

Damn the wretched accounts and bother David Nicholas! They were arriving in Ancient Greece, the legendary land of her childhood heroes and gods, and she must take it all in, because it was most unlikely that she would ever come this way again.

So she followed her tall companion like an obedient puppy as they emerged from the plane, her hazel eyes wide and senses reeling at the assault of so much splendour.

The surrounding hills were spectacularly bright, highlighted by the glaring sun, their drab brown and green burned-up vegetation a welcome darkness to the eye. Cicadas chirruped in the pine trees, a faint hint of subtle fragrance wafted from the flowering shrubs that lined the road, and everywhere the light was blindingly white. Annie breathed in great lungfuls of the heat-laden air and silently tried to memorise all that she saw.

"In you get." A car was waiting for them outside the airport and she climbed in while David said brief words of command to the minion who had met them, then removed his jacket before getting in beside her.

"We're driving straight to the ferry, won't take long," he remarked casually, but Annie was too overcome to answer.

The drive to the coast was, in fact, far too short in her humble opinion; besotted with the heat, the scent of thyme in the wind, and the mesmeric effect of the high hills beneath which they drove, she could hardly take it all in. But once at the port, where a chugging ferry waited, she realised that here was yet another sort of beauty.

The wind blowing off the Aegean was slapdash and mischievous, tugging at her bright hair and bringing a welcome coolness to a body already beginning to sag in the unaccustomed heat.

Once on board, deafened by the noisy voices all around her, and fascinated by the throbbing life of the little waterfront, she leaned against the rail, watching and listening, fascinated by all she saw.

"We'll have something to eat, and then I suggest you rest until we get to the island. And don't get sunburnt too quickly—"

David seemed to have shed much of his previous irritation and high-handedness as he smiled at her. He looked at home among ropes and spars and all the impediments of watercraft, thought Annie wistfully, suddenly recalling overheard stories of the long hours he spent on his yacht in various ports the world over, when he wasn't working. As he went off to organise a drink and some food, she followed his personable figure with her eyes, abrupt realism sharply pointing the enormous difference in their lives; she from a shared flat in London and he with homes in many countries . . . no wonder he had been put out at having to "make do" with her unworldly company, instead of that of Jill Martineau, who was as widely travelled and sophisticated as he was.

But such thoughts were only momentary, for she saw him returning with glasses and plates. They picnicked on prawn salad and fresh fruit washed down with ice-cool, real lemonade. The sun-drenched afternoon found Annie ready to huddle sleepily on the bleached boards of the ferry, leaning unconcernedly against a creaking bulwark, lulled to a stupor by the roar of the warm wind and the unfamiliar sensation of sun burning every part of her uncovered body.

When she awoke it was to hear the shrill toot-toot of the ferry announcing its arrival at the island. As she scrambled to her feet she discovered that David's jacket had been draped over her exposed shoulders—but there was no time to thank him, for excitement filled the boat, and along with the other passengers she dashed to the rail, finding him already there.

"Doloffinos." He glanced down at her, then nodded to the distant isle. Silent at his side, she watched the small green jewel

16

grow bigger and more beautiful, moment by moment.

As they drew nearer, Annie could see a little town of white houses, one perched seemingly upon another, stretching up the hillside and clustering around the waterfront. Alleys, narrow streets, cobbles, snatches of green creepers, of vivid blossoms, enchanted her curious eyes. The people thronging the waterside formed a veritable kaleidoscope of old women, dark suntanned men, girls with flashing eyes, handsome swarthy children and, of course, tourists.

Most seemingly international and moneyed, they filled the air with the purrings of their expensive cars, the variety of their native tongues, the blend of their couture perfumes—without doubt, thought Annie, wide-eyed, the jet set. Bronzed, tall and immaculately but casually dressed, they stood out against the purity and primitiveness of the island like filmic gods on a movie set.

She watched and wondered, seeing David's face expand as he exchanged greetings here and there—clearly, he was well-known in Doloffinos. Again, she was acutely reminded of the difference in their lives. Another car had appeared as if by magic, a blue open-topped little racer, and soon they were driving out of the town, along a dusty, winding road which followed the scalloped coastline, slowly climbing towards a green-tree'd headland a mile or so away.

At the end of a steep, narrow concrete track, huge gates bore the welcome sign— DOLOFFINOS HOLIDAY VILLA ESTATE. They had arrived! Annie caught her breath—so this was the reality of all the dreary figures she had studied in the report on the plane, this lovely, luxurious estate, shaded by stone pines and gnarled, silvery-grey olive trees, emblazoned with vivid geraniums hanging from walls and ornamental urns, with sprawling, purple climbers hanging on the fencing that separated the individual villas. And over all hung the fragrance of dried thyme in the warm air, wafted by a wind which made soulful music in the pines on the nearby headland.

She was tired, quite overcome by all she had seen, and so when David got out of the car, calling casually, "Well, come on, don't just sit there!", it was too much for her.

"Actually, I was waiting for you to help me," she returned icily, suddenly incapable of controlling the quick tongue which had been her downfall all her short life, and didn't wait to see the bleached eyebrows rise in amazement and disapproval, as she climbed nimbly out, preceding him up the path to the large white villa that confronted them.

But before she could look around her more fully, her eyes fell on something so distressing that immediately her mind had only one thought; dropping her bag, she hurried towards the wheelchair parked on the small paved terrace by the open french window, intent on comforting its small weeping occupant.

"Don't cry! It can't be as bad as all that! Is it your leg—does it hurt so much?"

Huge dark eyes stared up from a tear-stained, swarthy thin face, and the noisy sobs slowly died away. Annie smiled encouragingly, hands about the child's own sunburned paws. "However did you do it? Slipped on a banana skin, I bet . . ." She rapped gently on the brilliant white plaster which covered the extended right leg. "You've collected quite a few autographs, I see—may I add mine?" Fumbling in her shoulder bag for a pen, and quickly scribbling her name on the cast, she became aware that the little girl's tears had stopped, and that a faint smile lit her face.

"There you are, Annie Frayne." She grinned persuasively. "And what's your name? Do you speak English? I hope so, because I don't know a single word of Greek, even though I bought a dictionary before I left . . ."

A cold voice behind her took the smile from Annie's face.

"May I remind you that we're here to do a job of work and not just to amuse small invalid children, however tear-stained they may be?" David Nicholas put a masterful hand beneath her arm and heaved her up from the side of the wheelchair. Annie had the grace to flush, but stood her ground.

"Sorry, I was only making friends; it's one of the first things explorers in a strange land do, you know—"

He stared down at her with icy steel chips. "We'll discuss your views on exploration at some later date, Annie, if we must. Now come along in, Marcus will be waiting for us in the office."

"Yes, of course, Mr. Nicholas."

She followed him along the path from the terrace, towards the open door nearby, her eyes squinting in the brilliant sunshine, turning back once to wave at the small girl, who watched them.

"What did you say her name was, Mr. Nicholas?" Annie asked innocently as he stood back to allow her to enter.

"I didn't. But the girl is Marcus's daughter, Alexa. No doubt you'll see her again—from all I hear Marcus won't be parted from her for a moment. One reason why he's neglected his work, of course."

His face was grim as he dropped his bag on the polished floorboards in the spacious hall. "This way."

Annie followed him down the passage and into a large, airy office with whitewashed walls, cane furniture and vivid, flowery curtains that framed double windows opening on to a sunlit terrace. At the big desk dominating the room a stocky figure rose to his feet at their entrance, and she realised immediately that this was

Alexa's father, for the likeness was so remarkable.

A handsome man, thought Annie quickly, with good-looking, heavy features and splendid teeth, showing a gleam of gold as he smiled. Strangely, amongst all that swarthiness, she noticed his eyes were of the palest blue. Her attention returned quickly to David, who held out his hand over the desk and said, "Well, here we are, Marcus," in a surprisingly informal way, making her realise they must be old friends as well as business colleagues.

The Greek smiled back warmly and shook the offered hand until Annie thought it might fall off then he went around the desk, drawing David close and kissing him effusively on both cheeks.

"Ah, David, so good to see you again, it's been a long while, eh? And this time we're meeting because things are bad . . . you come very much as my boss, I know, to clear up all the trouble I cause . . . well, sit down, sit down, and I'll get you a drink." His eyes moved towards Annie and the big smile enfolded her gladly. "How do you do? I am Marcus Kalamares."

"Sorry; this is Annie Frayne, who's come along to help me." David had the grace to look slightly ashamed of his forgetfulness.

"Delighted to welcome you to Doloffinos, Miss Frayne." Marcus hung on to Annie's hand while he beamed down at her, and then suddenly dropped it, as his face fell tragically, and he turned away.

"That chestnut hair! Ah, reminds me of poor little Ourania . . . see, she is so tiny . . ." The rich voice fell into a husky, confidential tone. "David, I think I shall never get over Ourania's death. And the child—Alexa still hasn't recovered from the accident. She sits out there with her poor leg, always sad; the specialist says all should be well, but why does she still weep? Four months and a half now, and she should be free of her plaster, running about like she used to. Is it any wonder I cannot concentrate on the business? Well, well—enough for the moment. I'll get you that drink."

As he left the room Annie looked enquiringly at David. "Poor man! What a state he's in; so his wife died in an accident?"

23

"A shocking affair. Ourania was a lovely girl, and they were ideally suited. Seems that neither he nor Alexa can get over it. Of course, the Greeks are ridiculously emotional at the best of times, but—"

"So are most people in a situation like that," said Annie daringly, braving the disapproving stare that met her words.

"I hope you don't intend to get too involved with emotional matters while we're here, Annie—there's a hell of a lot of work to be done, and this isn't meant to be a holiday, you know."

Marcus returned with a tray of drinks before she could answer, and perhaps it was just as well, for the words that were all too ready to snap out in reply would have been rude and very much to the point.

Later, sipping ice-cold *limonada*, as Marcus told her the drink was called, into which, despite her protestations she suspected he had slipped a tot of gin, and listening to the two men discussing some of the more urgent matters demanding their attention, Annie slowly regained her self-control.

Of course, he was right; she mustn't let

her ever-ready sympathy run away with her. But, even so, need he have accused her of intending to malinger and waste time? That was extremely unfair. What a cold fish David Nicholas must be; buttoned-up and sure of himself, without a single kind thought in his whole make-up . . . Then she remembered the jacket carefully draped over her burning bare arm as she slept on the boat, and frowned perplexedly.

Perhaps there was a side to him that he didn't willingly reveal to strangers, a side that was more gentle and considerate. Annie thought it most unlikely. But then she recalled the office rumours about all his girlfriends, so surely there had to be a little love in the man somewhere?

The heat and the weariness of the long journey, coupled with the gin-laced drink, relaxed Annie to the point when she could have easily dropped off to sleep, even as the men talked. Her eyes were actually half-closed, as she daydreamed of David Nicholas turning into a freely smiling, attentive companion, instead of the old grouch he undoubtedly was. Suddenly his amused voice awoke her with a start.

"Wake up, Annie!"

She stared across the room, ashamed of her lapse. Yes, he was actually smiling at her, the sea-grey eyes momentarily friendly.

"I—I'm sorry, Mr. Nicholas, it must be the sun—"

Marcus's easy smile flashed out. "See how sleepy she looks! Like a little dormouse!"

"Don't be fooled, Marcus—she may look like a mouse, but under that frail exterior, believe me, she's as fierce as a man-eating tiger!"

Was this the hard man she had just been berating in her dreams? Annie gulped and sat up very straight. David rose and pulled her to her feet with a casual hand. "Come on, you obviously need a nice long siesta. I'll take you to your room. Is that your bag?"

She followed him down the long passage leading through the rambling buildings. Various doors opened off at intervals, and finally he ushered her into a small, sparsely-furnished room with a tiny balcony beyond the open shutters of the big window.

"Make yourself at home and have a rest. We'll meet again for a drink before dinner. I think you'll find all you want here."

Annie stared, bemused, at the pale walls and the highly polished floorboards, where colourful woven rugs echoed the brightness of lampshade and cotton bedcover. There was a built-in wardrobe and another small door beyond the single bed, opening into a bathroom. A dressing-table and a cane lounging chair completed the furnishings.

"It—it looks fine, thank you." She covered up a yawn and blushed as she met his amused eyes.

"A dormouse; yes, I think Marcus was right . . ." Turning, he went towards the door, suddenly pausing to look back at her, the smile switched off and a familiar, stern expression sending a flight of butterflies into her stomach. "A word of advice, Annie. You're young and inexperienced. So I suggest you don't get too involved with Marcus and his family."

Annie stared, taken aback, full of instant resentment. "Well, thanks for thinking of my well-being, but surely what I choose to do in my spare time is my own affair? And it just happens that I should definitely *like* to get to know Alexa better; Marcus hinted that she's upset, maybe insecure after the accident . . . perhaps I can cheer her up a little."

"I would have thought being a social worker was hardly up your street, my dear Miss Frayne . . ."

The ridicule in his voice was too much for her. She flushed angrily and allowed herself to say the first words that rushed into her mind.

"Well, you may be right, Mr. Nicholas, but I know two things; one is that I'm certainly not *your dear*, and the other is that people are infinitely more important than *businesses . . .*" The door slammed behind him and she busied herself with unpacking in order to forget the uneasiness that his grim expression had left her with.

2

WHEN Annie awoke, the first
thing she became conscious of
was the wind rushing through
the pine trees on the headland, just a
stone's throw from the villa; a gentle rising
and falling, full of music and feeling. She
rose and went out onto the tiny balcony,
looking about her with wondering eyes.

Beneath the house the Aegean Sea
hushed and shushed, mildly lapping the
long, curving beach that lay in a huge
scallop shell of silver-gold sand, backed
with grave gnarled olive trees slipping
down from the emerald-clad hills above.

But it was to the headland on the right
of the beach that her glance finally
returned, for this was the source of the
music she heard. Watching, she saw
the trees swaying and dancing as the
capricious wind came bouncing over the
waves and into their tangled canopies. *The
pines are singing*, she murmured to
herself, quite enchanted with the sound,

and knew that she would always remember the romantic music as being the very essence of this beautiful isle.

After showering she dressed quickly, noticing guiltily how long she had slept. Already the fiery sun was slipping down towards the sea-girt horizon, the sky stained with all the jewel colours of an artist's palette.

Fresh and attractive in a new apple-green cotton skirt and a cream shirt, she left her room, heading for the office. Would she find David there? And if so, what frame of mind would he be in? A little nervously she opened the door and looked inside. The big airy room was empty and uncertainty hit her. Perhaps she should have waited in her own room until someone fetched her? Then common-sense returned—*what nonsense, I'm not a guest.* As that wretched David Nicholas had so plainly inferred, she was here to work; all right, then, work she would.

She sat herself down in the big chair that Marcus had vacated, eyeing the desk, so untidily covered with papers, account books and files, and then tried to sort them out into some semblance of order. A huge ledger fell open as she shifted it from one side to the other and at once she was caught up in her familiar working world of figures. "Hmm," mused Annie sharply, suddenly sensing trouble, "now, this looks all wrong . . ."

She was immersed in her checking when footsteps sounded in the hall and Marcus's warm voice said urgently from the doorway, "But what are you doing, Miss Frayne? Those are *my* books!"

She glanced up, seeing the gleam of suspicion in his pale eyes, and knew at once that she must charm him away from any awkwardly belligerent thoughts. Smiling, she shut the book and got to her feet.

"Oh no, Marcus, they're my books, too! We belong to the same firm, don't we? And I'm here specially to help put things right—so please don't bawl me out on my first evening!"

She walked towards him. "Is it time to eat yet? I'm starving."

His face relaxed. Easily moved, versatile in his moods and attitudes, Annie instinctively analysed him as being a large small boy; and as a family-minded girl, she knew all about getting on with children. She laid a hand on his arm. "Where's the kitchen? Lead on, Macduff . . ."

"Macduff?" Grinning back, he followed her lead, allowing her to pull him into the hallway. "But who is this Macduff, Miss Frayne?"

"Never mind who—just try calling me Annie, will you, Marcus? Do we cook our own food? I'm fairly good at bangers and mash, but I doubt if I can cope with anything more exotic—golly, what a super kitchen, it'd be a treat to cook in here. But it's all ready—"

She paused in the doorway, causing Marcus to bump into her. His heavy arm went around her shoulder as he said softly, "Anthula left it for us, just cold chicken and salad. We'll carry it onto the terrace and eat there. I'll get the wine."

"That'll be lovely. Er—just the two of us, Marcus?"

Half-hidden in the larder, finding the wine, his voice drifted faintly back to her. "David is seeing friends. Won't be back this evening. Okay to try our local red wine, Annie?"

"Yes, of course, just fine." A surprising

feeling of disappointment gripped her. So David was out on the town already, was he? Chatting up some of those lovely expensive suntanned creatures in exotic clothes who had called *hi, David darling*, when they saw him get off the ferry . . . Annie sternly dismissed her unworthy thoughts, telling herself that David Nicholas could do just as he liked, she didn't care one little bit—why should she? After all, it wasn't as if he'd left her on her own; she and Marcus were about to dine *á deux* on the terrace in the moonlight. What more could a girl want?

The evening fell about them like a gentle velvet cloak, under a sky brilliant with stars. From her seat at the white wrought-iron table, Annie stared around her, seeing the island clothed in near-darkness. The scent of thyme seemed intensified and the song of the trees took on a deeper, more sensuous tone.

Marcus was an excellent and attentive companion, and before long she felt quite at home, sitting there eating her meal and telling him about her family and her home.

"I've got to go and buy postcards when

I have time off tomorrow, or they'll never speak to me again when I get back."

"You're a close family?"

"Very close. It's a nice, warm feeling, knowing everybody's rooting for you, no matter what."

"What is this rooting, then?" He refilled their glasses, despite Annie's refusal, and she laughed at the puzzled expression on his face.

"Your English is marvellous, but I don't suppose you've ever heard that word before—sounds like a lot of pigs, actually. But it just means they'll always understand what I do, always love me."

"Always love you." He repeated the words softly, thoughtfully, and then smiled deep into her eyes. "That I know about. It is how we Greeks live—but I thought you English were supposed to be so cold?"

The wine was giving her a lovely floaty feeling; it made her tongue a little too loose. "Like David Nicholas, you mean?"

Marcus's deep pools of eyes widened. "David? Cold?" He roared with spontaneous laughter. "Oh no, Annie you're wrong. David is warm—passionate. How can you possibly say he's cold?"

"Quite easily." She ate the last slice of the big, juicy tomato on her plate with reluctance and looked hopefully at the basket of fresh fruit at the side of the table. "He's about as warm as a snake. Cold-blooded and only thinking of the wretched business."

"So you have had a fight, you two—yes, I think so." Marcus removed their empty plates and pushed the fruit basket towards her. Annie's fingers hovered over a large sun-kissed orange, then moved on to an even more tempting peach.

"This looks gorgeous . . . no, of course we haven't had a fight. How could we? He's the boss, I'm just an underling." She caught the question on his face. "Beneath him. Inferior. Or so he thinks—well, we shall see. Marcus, this peach is pure heaven; I think I might stay here for ever and live on salad and peaches . . ."

"And sleep on the beach, swim naked in the warm sea, become a child of nature? I would like to see that, Annie."

His giant hand slid over the table, covering her idle fingers. Startled, she looked up to find his eyes full of obvious admiration. "Well, I—er—I don't think I'll go that far, thanks. I burn too easily in the sun and I like a comfortable bed, so maybe I'll stay as I am—a well-behaved, conventional English ice-maiden." Removing her hand she made her smile a little less uninhibited, hoping he would accept the warning in her foolish words. Of course, she might have realised how dangerous the situation was—the romantic setting, the wine and the moonlight; all this was enough to set off any lusty Greek who found himself entertaining a girl on her own. Yes, she really must be more careful in future.

David's voice rang through her floaty head. *Young and inexperienced.*

"Oh damn him!" Annie said to herself testily. "Is the man always right?"

She would make sure he didn't find out about this little episode with Marcus. Too easily could she imagine the mockery in the grey-green eyes, the satisfaction in the deep, arrogant voice. *I told you so.*

To her great relief Marcus took the hint she had thrown out. Fetching coffee from the kitchen, while she arranged herself decorously in a cane lounger which she moved as far away as possible from the other chairs on the terrace while he was out of the way, he returned looking suitably serious, poured her coffee and sat at a discreet distance.

"You tell me of your family, now I tell you of mine. About my lovely Ourania, and my poor Alexa."

His liquid voice held her entranced. The tale was sad and she realised that, although he might easily dally with any girl who cared to play along, he would always sincerely mourn his beloved Ourania.

"So who looks after Alexa while you're working, Marcus?"

"My mother and my unmarried sister, Katnina. But most I have Alexa here with me—she can be moved in her chair wherever I go on the estate, and the people staying in the villas are kind. But she doesn't improve—no, no, even after the last operation, which cost so much."

Abruptly he stopped, stirred his coffee and changed the subject. "You must come and meet my family. My mother will like to see you, and my little brothers; and Katnina too, although . . ."

"Although what, Marcus?"

He stared at her through the half-light, the rising smoke from his cigar wreathing his face for a moment so that she couldn't see his eyes to make out what he was thinking. His voice, when finally he replied, was light and casual. "Although she is very busy. She helps Mama by day and works at night. More coffee, Annie?"

"No thanks, that was lovely. Yes, I'd like to meet your family. Do they live far away?"

"Just up the hillside. My father was a fisherman until he was drowned; now my brother Yannos works the boat. He is married and lives further along the coast. It is a hard life, fishing. The sea is beautiful on a night like this, calm, kindly, but it is a monster, as well. We of the island have to live with the monster to earn our living. But things are better for us now that we have tourists visiting—now that we have the estate."

Annie was intrigued, her thoughts suddenly raising deeper issues about the unfairness of human conditions. David Nicholas and his yacht—Marcus and his family fishing to keep away starvation.

"You mean that without the holiday trade you'd be very poor, Marcus?"

"Of course. That is how the island has always been. Now we may not always like the strangers coming, but we welcome the money they bring. We are polite to them."

"I see. So when you're being extra polite to me I shall know that all you're after is my money—yes?" She thought it was time to lighten the conversation; the wine had made her sleepy and bed was an attractive idea.

"No, no! People like you and David will always be welcome to us! Why, David and I are blood-brothers . . . we swore an oath when we were small and sealed it with our blood." Marcus made a dramatic gesture over his wrist, fine eyes flashing with humour and Annie shivered enjoyably, her interest suddenly recharged.

"I don't believe it! You mean you cut your wrists and mingled your blood? How splendid! Just like one of those old films!"

"But Greece *is* an old film—the oldest of them all, Annie. You have a lot to learn about us, I see."

"I'm sure I have. And I'm intrigued

about David being so close to you—do tell me, Marcus . . ."

He spun a smoke circle with deliberate slowness and then spoke in a voice full of lazy nostalgia. "David and I grew close when we spent our summers together as small boys. His father had a holiday cottage near ours, in the old days before the estate developed, and David was an only child. He had no one else to play with and his stepmother didn't seem to care about him . . . My older brother Yannos was always too busy to play, he worked with my father in the boat, so Katnina and I spent our time with David. We fished and swam and looked after the pigs and chicken and goats. Some days David painted—he is very clever with pictures. We picked grapes and olives in the autumn, and we told each other exciting tales of the old gods when we sat around a fire on the beach, cooking what we had caught that day. Ah yes, to be young— it was a good time. And David and Katnina—"

He stopped suddenly, stubbing out his cigar and rising, putting a hand under Annie's arm to help her up. "But that's enough of the old days, I sound like a grandfather! Now I must go and see my little Alexa before she sleeps. Tomorrow you will come and visit us, Annie, tomorrow when the work is done. I will take you home with me; you would like that, yes?"

"I'd love it, Marcus. Thank you."

"My pleasure, Annie."

He stood very close to her, so close that she could smell the evocative fragrance of the cigar, the headiness of the wine on his breath. Uncertainly she paused, not sure whether to run—they were alone here and already Marcus had demonstrated how quickly his sensuality could be aroused. He lifted a hand and stroked her hair, and her fright disappeared as she watched his eyes slowly fill with tears.

"So like my Ourania. Oh, Annie, Annie . . ."

She stepped away quickly. Things were moving too fast. David had said not to get too involved, now she knew how right he had been. Smiling brightly and breathing a sigh of relief at having escaped a more serious attempt at casual seduction, Annie went back into the hallway, glancing over her shoulder and feigning a yawn as Marcus reluctantly followed her.

"Goodness, is that really the time? I had no idea it was so late—think I'll have an early night. Thanks for looking after me so well, Marcus—see you tomorrow."

"But Annie—" He sounded crestfallen and she chuckled to herself as she retreated to her own room, turning the key once she got inside and closing the shutters against the night.

As she lay in bed the day's happenings unreeled before her eyes. So much that was new and surprising, so much beauty that touched her in a strange, painful way, deep down inside. Annie took a longer time than usual to go to sleep because her mind was over-busy, but at last she slid down the long, fuzzy slope towards oblivion, her last conscious thought being of David Nicholas.

Maybe the fact that he was an only son, with an uncaring stepmother, might account for his seemingly forbidding outward manner. But—warm and passionate, Marcus had said . . .

In the morning all was noise and bustle

around the estate and Annie had no time in which to stand and wonder at the glory of the new day she glimpsed from the window when she threw it open.

The freshly washed splendour of the beach below the hillside, the sorrowfulness of the sad, strange song of a grazing mule, all must wait until David Nicholas deigned to give her official time-off in which to delight in such things, she told herself firmly, even forgetting to listen for the music in the pine trees, for Anthula had knocked at her door early, calling that there was tea in the kitchen and breakfast would be ready very shortly.

Dressed in a respectable cotton dress which covered her uncomfortably burning shoulders and arms, bare legs slipped into flipflop sandals, Annie felt ready to face this new and exciting world.

In the kitchen she drank a welcome mug of tea, then helped herself to rolls and butter and honey, fresh fruit, and a giant cup of coffee, while exchanging brief English-cum-Greek words and friendly smiles with Anthula, the middle-aged maid, finally taking her tray out onto the terrace where male voices already warned her that David and Marcus were about.

David glanced her way. "Morning," he said casually. "Ready for work?"

She opened her mouth to say *of course,* but had no chance to speak as immediately he turned back to Marcus to continue the conversation she had interrupted. She sat alone with her breakfast, wondering crossly whether this sort of matter-of-fact treatment would last all the time she was here. She felt vaguely like a schoolgirl, uncertain of her status, yet longing for a chance to show how grown-up and competent she really was.

The chance soon came. David drained his coffee, got to his feet and came towards her. She looked up, mouth full of roll and honey, suddenly unaccountably overawed by the magnetic presence of the man who towered over her. She thought that David's hair seemed even brighter today, as if the sun had welcomed back an old and valued friend; he wore pale shorts and a dark green shirt decorated with silver Greek key pattern. His bare arms and legs were tanned almost as brown as Marcus's body, and the fuzz of golden hairs on his arms shone like a discreet halo, accentuating his masculinity and undeniable attraction.

"How's the dormouse?" he asked with a look of barely concealed amusement on his face.

Annie hiccupped and felt her cheeks flame. "Sorry. I mean, I wasn't—I didn't . . ."

"I'm sure you didn't. You'll have to keep out of the sun today." He ran a finger lightly down her burning arm and she felt herself erupt in strange tingles of pleasure. "Not that you'll have time to do anything else but work anyway." The amusement disappeared, and was replaced by the familiar stern expression.

Annie fidgetted and dropped her eyes, hating him for causing her to feel so exactly like the schoolgirl she definitely wasn't.

"Marcus and I are going around the estate this morning and later in the afternoon we have an appointment at the bank down in the village. I think you'll have more than enough to keep you busy while I'm away. Have a rest after lunch, by all means, but I should definitely like you to sort out that ledger today, even if it means working on a bit. All right, my dear Miss Frayne?"

Being called his dear Miss Frayne was devastating after his former friendliness, because for some reason it made her see herself as a mere cog in his vast machine, and for even more obscure reasons, which she didn't feel capable of analysing, she was determined to make him realise she was infinitely more than just a cog . . .

"All right, Mr. Nicholas." She watched him leave the terrace. Marcus paused at her side, looking strained and apologetic.

"I'm sorry, Annie—the visit to my home must wait. Maybe tomorrow. Today is—well, you see how today is . . ." He nodded resignedly and left her, and in a moment she heard the sound of a car driving away through the estate.

Alone with the books in the office, she sat and stared mutinously at the almost illegible entries. What on earth had Marcus been up to these last few months? There had been obvious discrepancies in the accounts she had studied in the plane coming over and it looked now as if they were still continuing. And why had he never bothered to make his work clearer and more easily understandable? Now, that five looked remarkably like a nine . . .

Hours later, during which time she retreated into her own magical work-world of enjoyable figure analysis, Anthula tapped on the door and said, "Lunch on terrace, Annie. I come back to cook dinner. Marcus and David out all day."

Annie had a solitary salad and took her coffee back to the office, where she continued working until the overpowering heat and accompanying lassitude made her head reel, her eyelids falter. Recognising defeat, she went to her room. Sleep came instantly and no dreams hindered her peaceful siesta.

When she awoke she resolutely returned to the office; it was important that David should find her at the desk when he came back. Clearly, he considered her an irresponsible worker who must be shouted at and told exactly what to do, for how long, and when. Annie's mind seethed at the idea, but soon the figures again took over and she was amazed to find, as she finally resolved some of the muddled and ill-written entries, that the day was ending, the sun slipping down, and that she was nursing a pounding headache through too much heat and overwork.

There was no sign of anybody around; only a few of the villa people, driving in and out of the gates, either coming home after a day on the beach, or leaving to have supper at one of the nearby tavernas. For a moment she felt uncharacteristically depressed. She hadn't realised she would be left all alone like this, on her first day. But with the thought, determination won through the gloom. She would go for a walk—yes, fresh air was just what she needed. The hillside, or the beach?

"The pines—I'll go and explore the pines."

Only stopping to change her short-sleeved dress for jeans and a covered-up shirt—last night's airing on the terrace had taught her a thing or two about evening forays by hungry mosquitoes—she followed the track towards the headland, which joined the path running from the road up to the villa gates. Annie swung along, senses immediately charged high with the fragrance of the burnt thyme bushes and the lulling music of the pine trees. What a place!

Her near-depression of earlier in the evening had completely disappeared. By now even David Nicholas's well-known mercurial changes of temperament had ceased to annoy her. For here, among the tall trees, was peace and beauty enough to give her new serenity.

A pale, diffused green light filtered through the spreading branches, cooling her and recalling walks in the damp, lush English countryside with the family, when she still lived at home. Thoughts of the beloved family reminded her that, come what may, David or no David, tomorrow she really must get to the village and buy those postcards. What an old misery he was, to make her work so hard today.

The path meandered on through the trees, with here and there an occasional, tempting glimpse of the sea below the headland, fiery now in its reflection of the spectacular sunset that surmounted it. Annie fingered the smooth boles of the trees and stopped to inspect a flower. Foolishly she smiled at it, listening to the mysterious music of the wind, her thoughts delightfully at ease.

Suddenly a small building loomed up, and she saw a wooden cabin emerge through the trees. How interesting! Who would live here, right on the headland, hidden away like this?

It only took a moment to see that the cabin was deserted, but that someone had undoubtedly lived here once. The door swung open invitingly on a broken hinge, and she tiptoed in, eyes alert for signs of recent habitation, but finding none. Twigs and fallen leaves littered the bare floorboards and cobwebs hung over smudgy windows where, clearly, last winter's storms had lashed. The huge window at the far side of the cabin, she discovered, looked out into a small clearing, with a rough track descending to a tiny cove below.

Transfixed suddenly by the sense of space after the claustrophobic atmosphere of the enclosing trees, Annie just stood and stared. The sea was fiery red, streaked with darker, subtle colours, reflected from the overwhelming backdrop of the sunset. The beauty made her catch her breath—

then her wandering eyes fell on a shadowy blur on the beach below—a boat lying on its side on the mysteriously veiled sand. Small cream-flecked waves rose and fell and Annie felt herself being lulled by the twin voices of sea and wind.

Marcus's words came back to her, bringing with them a strange sense of disquiet. *A monster we have to live with.* She turned away with a shiver; he was right, water could be so treacherous.

She looked around the cabin with increasing interest. Gradually it became clear to her that the place must belong to an artist—canvases were piled against the wooden walls, one or two hanging where the light was strongest. She looked at them curiously, peering through the half-light. Mostly land and seascapes, they spoke to her at once with a depth of feeling and love of colour with which she could easily identify.

One picture in particular held her gaze; she could almost feel the cool freshness of the breaking waves against the scalloped shoreline; the intense heat of the midday sun baking sparse earth rockhard. Yes, she liked it; he was talented, this artist. She

51

knew instinctively he was a man, for the strength and sensuality in the pictures was undeniably male.

The one square room of the cabin held all that was necessary for basic living, she saw—a table, holding dirty plates, glasses and the litter of paint tubes and brushes, some rough cane chairs, shelves filled with books and more paints, a camping gas-cooker and a big, cracked stone sink with a couple of buckets beneath it.

And a couch . . .

Annie chuckled. The couch was entirely out of keeping with the rest of the rather drab room; voluptuously covered with vivid coloured hangings and cushions, it looked like something out of a French bedroom farce. She walked over and tested its comfort. Not bad—a bit saggy in the middle, but no doubt that was because of all the artist's models it had accommodated . . . grinning at her own imagination she adjusted a cushion behind her head and lay at ease, surveying the scene around her.

Only then did she see the enormous portrait that hung at the end of the cabin, opposite the couch, half-hidden in shadows. By now used to the failing light, she stared at it curiously. Obviously painted by the same artist as the land and seascapes, this was a much more ambitious work.

The girl in the portrait was a beauty with a shield-shaped face and vital, gleaming dark eyes. Bare arms and magnificent breasts rose from the heavy cleavage of a scarlet dress of rich, brocaded material, skilfully highlighted by the painter.

Annie shivered abruptly. There was so much animal attraction in the figure that she felt uncomfortable, lying on the couch staring at it. Especially as she realised that the artist himself must have hung the portrait on that wall so that he, too, could lie here and gaze at it . . . instinctively she swung her legs over the edge of the couch. Time to go. This place was haunted, alive with an atmosphere which troubled her in some inexplicable way.

As her feet touched the boards, there was a sound in the open doorway, and a beam of light flashed in, sweeping around the cabin, finding her and transfixing her, like a butterfly on a pin. Annie gasped and cowered back on the couch.

"Ah!" said a familiar voice. "So the dormouse has found another nest. Sorry if I frightened you, my dear Miss Frayne. But this *is* my property, you know."

Annie let out her pent-up breath in a huge sigh of relief and was about to stand up and start apologising when, with quick strides David was beside her, one hand on her shoulder, restraining her.

"Don't get up, you look so cosy there." He sat down beside her on the couch, putting the torch on a shelf by the headboard, and smiled into her taut face. "So you've found my hideaway . . ."

"I—I had a headache and I thought a walk would help—" She gulped and ended weakly, "Yes, I've found it."

"Like it?"

"Oh, yes." She slid an assessing glance at his face, saw his amiable smile and was encouraged to add, "I didn't know you were a painter. I like your work very much. It's real."

"Why, thank you, Annie. I don't have much time for it nowadays, only when I'm on holiday, or slipping off for a weekend . . . I was down in the cove with my boat just now and thought I'd better look in here on the way up and see what sort of a mess it's got into. Didn't realise you were having a siesta." His eyes were alive with friendly mockery, and she felt her spirits reviving, her fears going.

"So that was your boat? I saw it from the window. Do you keep a boat in all your estate homes?"

"Like a girl in every port? But of course!" He grinned wickedly at her. "Like to come out in it one day?"

"Yes, please—but only if the sea's calm." Marcus's warning rang in her head.

"No need to be worried. I'm a competent sailor, you know."

He looked exactly that, she thought, taking in the oilstained teeshirt and faded jeans rolled half-way up his legs.

"I should think you're competent in everything you do," she commented unthinkingly, and was totally unprepared for his reaction.

"Practice makes perfect, little mouse." Suddenly his arms were around her, his face only a breath away. She smelt the tang of salt and the faint smokiness of occasional cigars; then his lips touched hers, lightly, gently, butterfly-kissing caressing her cheeks, her throat, slipping slowly down towards the open v-neck of her shirt.

Annie resisted with all her might. She was hardly a newcomer to the welcome casual kiss, but this was something different. They were alone here in the half-lit darkness of a hidden cabin; and she knew instinctively that if she allowed herself to stay, David's well-practised earthy charm and attraction could easily lead to her downfall. And that must never happen.

With all her puny might she fought to free herself. Surprisingly he gave in with good grace.

"So the mouse has turned into that damned tiger again—all right, Annie, no more games tonight. Let's go back and have something to eat before we turn in. We've got a hard day before us tomorrow."

Casually he hauled her to her feet, picked up the torch and led the way out of the cabin, up through the heavy darkness of the pines and along the track to the villa, standing white in the moonlight above them.

Annie followed in his footsteps, dazed and bruised, not by the sweet, light kisses, but by the unexpectedness of the casual return to normality of the man.

No more games tonight . . .

So he thought she was the sort of girl who was ready for a meaningless flirtation, did he? Oh, but how wrong he was.

3

WHEN Annie awoke next morning, her immediate thoughts were of the previous evening. As she showered, then dressed, she recalled the resentment that had sprung to life once she and David had entered the villa, for the dinner she shared with him and Marcus had been dominated by the men's business talk. She might have been a mere fly on the wall for all the notice they took of her. Once the plates were emptied and the sweet-smelling cigars lit, wafting pale circles of smoke into the velvety night sky, she had taken herself off to bed.

"Please excuse me, I'm tired."

David had scarcely looked up, just lifted an uncaring hand to wave in her direction, but Marcus rose, following her off the terrace and putting his hand on her arm before she disappeared towards her room.

"Goodnight, Annie—you've had a dull day, I'm afraid; business, nothing but business, eh?" His philosophical shrug and friendly, concerned smile thawed some of the irritation within her and she smiled back.

"I understand, Marcus. Don't worry about it."

He came a step nearer, eyes like deep pools, fathomless and profound. "But we make up for it tomorrow, yes?" An expression of comical secretiveness slid over his face as he winked at her and lowered his deep, resonant voice. "We slide off together, eh? David has many things to see to, he will be thinking of them, not of us . . ."

Too weary to demur, she nodded. David's total absorption in the business irked her, even as she accepted that it was an admirable trait—but it would be fun to show him that she was a person in her own right and not merely the naive little English mouse he thought her to be. So yes, she would definitely assert herself by accepting Marcus's invitation to meet his family tomorrow.

"I'd like that Marcus, it'll be lovely. Well, goodnight now . . ."

The morning was even more beautiful than

she could have imagined, the stretching sable sands below newly washed and fringed by tiny waves that scalloped the beach with an edging of fine, creamy lace. Annie ate her breakfast alone at the edge of the terrace, dazed with the splendour of the landscape.

Back in the office half an hour later, David appeared dressed in a conventional dark suit, frowning as he pushed files and papers into a gold-monogrammed brief-case. He took no notice of Annie, looking beyond her to where Marcus hovered at the filing cabinet.

"I'm flying to Athens to see the accountants, don't know how long they'll keep me. They're being bloody-minded about the accounts, damn them. You've got a lot to answer for, Marcus, one way or the other."

He sounded unpleasantly angry and Annie held her breath as the men scowled at each other across the room. Marcus said, with a stiff kind of dignity, "I apologise. But we all make mistakes."

"Mistakes?" David shut the case with an irate snap of the lock and stared over Annie's bowed head. "I've got a nasty feeling that it's not only mistakes that have fouled up the accounts—and if that's so, then God help you, my friend, for I shan't be able to."

Mutual animosity filled the hot, sunny room and Annie wished she was elsewhere. Wanting to break the atmosphere, she broke in impulsively, "—but there *are* mistakes, I found several yesterday while I was checking, silly things like incorrect addition and—"

"—and you can just keep out of this, thanks. If I want your advice I'll ask for it." David's hard eyes and forceful words silenced her, sending the colour rushing to her cheeks.

She watched him stride out of the room, letting the door slam behind him, heard his footsteps crunch out into the garden, and finally watched the blue car race away towards the village and the distant airport, suppressed violence all too evident in the scream of hot tyres on the dusty cement road.

Marcus sat down heavily in David's big chair and sighed. Then his eyes alighted on Annie's averted face and, feeling them upon her, she looked up, watching his frown relax into a beaming smile as he got up and came to her side.

"David and I fight, and not for the first, or possibly the last time—but it's done now. We have the day to ourselves, eh, Annie? Come, let's do the round of the villas and see what complaints our fussy holiday-makers can dream up today!"

"But the work?" Annie indicated the heavy books and files that littered the desk, a little aghast at his easy disregard of his responsibilities here.

"We'll do it later when the sun goes down; when we've had a happy visit to my home and then cooled off with a swim." He caught the doubt on her face and nodded reassuringly. "Yes, I mean it— tonight we'll work very hard and get everything cleared up. We'll surprise David when he returns tomorrow—or the next day—and then we'll be friends again, you'll see; no more fighting."

It was on the tip of her tongue to enquire just what would happen if David's visit to the accountants revealed further discrepancies, or even apportioned a defi- nite blame, but Marcus's eyes were as appealing as a dog asking for a run in the park, and she hadn't the heart to deny him.

"Well, all right—but who'll run the office while we're away?"

"Anthule takes messages. There's no hurry, we'll sort things out later, this evening, tomorrow, perhaps . . . the estate runs itself, don't look so worried. Everything will be all right."

He really was a hopeless manager, she told herself, as she followed him around the villas, hailing the occupants with friendly charm and assuring them that their little queries and complaints would all be dealt with.

"Just enjoy your holiday, we'll do the rest. Yes, yes, of course—I'll send someone to look at the plumbing straight away . . ."

By midday she discovered that, although she found Marcus a likeable and charming man, her business sympathies were definitely with David. "Hadn't we better get back and deal with one or two things now?" she asked, as they paused by a low oleander hedge over which a delectable slice of scenery presented itself.

Marcus sniffed the air enjoyably. "Poh,

poh, poh, don't worry so much, Annie . . . the tide's turned, just right for a swim." He smiled at her anxious face. "It's all right! I'll leave a note at the handyman's cottage about Madame Freya's toilet, and the broken shutter at the last villa—we have nothing to worry about now, the work's done for the day! A swim, some lunch, and then a siesta . . ."

"And then some work in the office," finished Annie resolutely, but unable to keep her face straight. What a spoilt child he was! And of course it would be lovely to cool off in that gorgeous blue-green water that lapped so invitingly, down there on the silver beach . . .

She followed him down the path, pushing aside the thought that David would be furious—and rightly so—if he knew what went on directly his back was turned. At this point her own guilt filled her with a sense of reluctant remorse, but then she remembered his uncaring, almost rude, attitude to her presence here, and thought grimly that she was doing no more than getting a bit of her own back; clearly he had no opinion of her, expecting her to be only a liability and a malingerer . . .

well, just for once she would live up to those dubious expectations, and be damned to the great David Nicholas!

The sea received her hot body with caressing coolness. Wading through the miniature waves into deeper water, she felt the disconcerting uneasiness that David's row with Marcus had called forth falling away from her, like raindrops from an oiled surface.

How utterly beautiful it was here, with the gentle turquoise-tinted water bearing her up as she ducked her head, wide eyes gradually becoming used to the saltiness as she searched the translucent depths, seeing here a slender weed swaying in the slight current, there a quivering, quicksilver fish darting out of sight.

Without any warning, the serenity of the underwater world was shattered. A shape approached her, darkly menacing, and she thrust for the surface, as strong hands gripped hers, dragging her further into the shadowy depths. With her lungs nearly bursting and her heart hammering wildly, Annie suddenly realised this was no fishy monster of Greek mythology, but merely

Marcus, playing the natural games of one reared in an island community.

Kicking herself away, she soared out of his reach and burst back into the hot, sunlit world above, sucking in air gratefully and forgetting her fright, inclined to laugh instead at such little-boy antics.

Then a sleek, dark head popped up beside her and Marcus threw the glistening swathe of hair out of his eyes. "Nearly got you!" he spluttered gleefully, "but you slipped through my hands like a little fish . . ." Swimming closer he reached out a hefty arm but Annie backed away, treading water at a safe distance and fixing him warningly with her eyes.

"Please don't ever do that again, Marcus. No, *no*. . . !" She pushed him off as he bent over her, eyes twinkling, his huge smile flashing out with obvious delight.

"You don't like it? You mean, you don't want to play, down there?" Slowly, realisation hit him and he dropped back, frowning at her suddenly with comic disbelief.

Annie felt she had let him down. "I'm sorry," she said meekly, "but I thought I was drowning, I couldn't get my breath. Leave me alone, please, Marcus—I'm not the waterbaby that you are, you see . . ."

He nodded slowly. "I forget Annie, you're English."

"—And therefore different! Well, you're right, I suppose." She grinned a little wryly and then wished she hadn't relaxed her defences, as Marcus's arms abruptly pulled her to him in a bearlike hug.

"I look after you. I will be your big brother and keep you safe."

But the salt kiss he deposited on her surprised mouth was no brotherly salute. Annie wrenched herself away, hitting out at him, her temper suddenly ignited by her own quick reactions. First David, and now this great wet monster out of the depths, both trying to inveigle her into "playing games" . . .

"Stop it!" she shouted indignantly, and turning her back on him performed the quickest crawl of her life to the safety of the shore. By the time she had towelled her hair and dried her face, her temper had burned itself out. Marcus strode up the beach and dripped all over her nicely

67

drying bikini as she lay on the burning sand, his eyes full of contrition.

"Annie, forgive me, I was only playing, I didn't mean any harm. You see, here on the island the sea is our natural playground, so I thought—"

"I know, Marcus, you just thought I was a nice new playmate. Well, I'm not." But, in spite of herself, she smiled forgivingly at him. Such a child; impossible to dislike such spontaneity and genuine friendliness. "It's all right, I understand. But no more games, okay?"

Looking crestfallen, he turned away to reach his towel. "No more games," he agreed sadly.

Annie closed her eyes against the blinding glare of the sun and abruptly recalled David's voice saying the same three words. Disconcertingly she was filled with a sudden and unfamiliar physical need.

Would she have pushed David away if he had been the one to kiss her, out there in the salty, buoyant water? Tingling, aghast at this new revelation of thought, she pushed away the idea and sat up quickly, wiping the lingering grains of hot sand from her body.

"Let's go, shall we, Marcus? I expect Alexa is waiting for us—didn't you say she was at home with your mother today?"

Ignoring the surprise on his face she slid into her jeans and shirt, feeling the cotton scraps of her bikini already dry, such was the force of the sun. Without looking back she gathered up her towel and walked up the beach into the welcome shade of the towering stone pines.

"You're cross, Annie?" Marcus caught her up within minutes, and the naive curiosity in his voice made her turn, smiling back at him under the heavy swing of her still-damp hair.

"Of course not. Just a bit . . ." She paused, considering the bewildering emotions that throbbed just beneath the surface.

Just a bit confused, to tell the truth; confused and unsure of herself. Aware, too, in a totally new way of David Nicholas, a man who had first irritated her and now kept intruding into her mind with a recurrence that was worrying—in fact, more than a little frightening. She met

Marcus's eyes and came back to reality. "Just a bit touched by the sun, I think!"

He responded at once to her lighter tone. "Ah, you pale, cold English girls! You need to keep out of the sun at first. It burns, it weaves a spell, I warn you. Come, you'll be safe now, we go up through the trees to my home. Alexa will be waiting, as you say. And I tell you what —you shall go by mule!"

"Oh, no!"

"Oh, yes!" He was quite imperturbed, passing her and grabbing her rolled-up towel to carry with his own, leading her through the trees and up a small side-track to a shabby stone cottage tucked into the green hillside, where a couple of sad-eyed mules stood, nose to tail beneath an olive tree.

He shouted a greeting and an old man appeared, smiling toothlessly. For a few minutes they conversed and then one of the mules was saddled, ready for her journey up the mountain.

"Up you get!" Marcus's brawny arms siezed her without ceremony, bundling her onto the hard wooden seat.

As they moved off, Annie turned and

waved at the old man, who, in his grubby white shirt and wide hat tipped over a beaky nose, silently watched them climb towards the hazy-green forest covering the mountain ahead of them.

Once she was used to the awkward roll of the mule's unwilling gait, and the hardness of the cumbersome saddle, Annie began to enjoy herself. The sun, near its zenith, was fiercely hot, but the canopy of leaves overhead provided welcome dappled shade. The path before them unwound, ever climbing, and Annie felt herself relax into the mule's uneven roll. Refreshed by the coolness, her thoughts took a happier turn and she smiled down at Marcus, whose brown hand grasped the animal's bridle. "This is fun! I'm really enjoying myself."

He looked up, answering her spontaneous smile. "Not far now—are you hungry? Mmm . . ." He sniffed the air like a hungry bear. "I can smell Mama's cooking already!"

"Oh, Marcus, you're such a clown!"

"No, no, I'm quite serious. Fish stew, an old family recipe made specially for you. Prawns, garlic, squid . . ." He kissed his fingers dramatically, blue eyes alive with enjoyment and Annie shook her head, amused and somehow touched by his simplicity.

Why couldn't David be like this, she thought—fun, easy to get on with, honest and sincere. But already they were approaching a clearing in the trees, and there was Alexa's eagerly pathetic face staring down the path from where she sat in her wheelchair outside the open doorway of a small white stone cottage.

"Papa!"

Marcus lengthened his stride and in a moment was bending over her, kissing her upraised face, while the mule came to a halt beside him.

"A visitor for you, Alexa—this is Annie, who comes all the way from Britain—but I forgot, you met the other day . . ." With the leading rein still in his hand, he lifted Annie from the saddle.

Rubbing her bottom she grimaced humorously. "That's better! I've never been on such a hard seat." Then, turning she went down on her knees beside the chair. "How are you, then, Alexa? I've been so looking forward to seeing you again."

Huge, sombre eyes returned a shy smile. "Hallo, *Thespinis*—" Alexa looked back at her father and began to gabble away in her own language. Marcus hitched the mule to a branch and went to fetch water from the well in the courtyard bordering the cottage, answering her over his shoulder. "You must speak English, Alexa —good practice for you. Annie doesn't know any Greek."

"Then I will try—"

Annie took the small hands in her own. "Call me Annie, won't you? I hope we can be friends." She groped in her shoulderbag. "Look, this is for you." It was only a phial of frosted cologne, bought hurriedly in the supermarket at home before she left England, but by the sudden gleam in the child's eyes, it might have been a jewel of pure gold.

"Oh, thank you . . . how lovely!"

Marcus returned, smoothing her dark hair with a loving gesture. "Tomorrow the plaster comes off," he said to Annie, "and then she will walk again . . ." Suddenly his face was unfamiliar, for the loving expression filling it as he turned back to Alexa was a very private one, meant for his daughter alone. Annie felt a lump come into her throat, as father and child smiled at each other in complete love and trust.

Then abruptly—"Come now!" Marcus was himself again, wheeling the chair in through the doorway, shouting for his mother as he did so. "We smelt the dinner as we came up the mountain! Mama! Come and meet our visitor. Spyro, Georgious, where are you?"

Swarthy faces appeared from the interior of the cottage, dark eyes bright and curious. Annie blinked as she left the glare of the sun behind, following Marcus and Alexa indoors.

An elderly, plump woman, with bent shoulders and a warm smile that over-rode the many wrinkles, took her hand and nodded a greeting. "Please to come in." The heavily-accented words were echoed by the young boys at her side. "Come in, come in . . ." A chair scraped and Annie sat down, feeling strangely at home.

It was cool here, she thought gratefully,

cool and welcoming, with only the basic requirements of life furnishing the small, square kitchen. The earth floor supported white-washed walls, along which stood cupboards and a fridge. A scrubbed table stretched from one end to the other with its surrounding chairs, and on the opposite side of the room was an electric cooker beside a primitive stone sink. And beyond that, of all unexpected things, thought Annie with surprise, was a television set. Not liking to appear blatantly curious about her surroundings, she concentrated on trying to return the messages of friendliness that shone from the dark, watchful eyes of Marcus's family.

"It's so kind of you to invite me to come."

The youngest boy leaned over the table, eagerness underlined by his restless, drumming fingers and quick words. "You watch football in Britain, *Thespinis?*"

"Football?" Taken aback, Annie glanced at Marcus as he lifted Alexa into the chair beside his at the top of the table. He raised an eyebrow despairingly.

"Georgious is crazy about it—last week

he saw Manchester United on television and it's all he can think about now."

Annie smiled understandingly at the merry-eyed boy. "My brother's just the same, but he's a fan of Argyle . . ."

"Argyle? Oh, no, not so good, they don't win too often!"

"Georgious." A quiet word from his mother silenced him, and he left the table to fetch bowls from the cupboard.

"And are you a football fan, too?" Annie asked the older boy. He shook his head, grinning in a way that declared his contempt for childish things.

"Spyro has no time for that, he works on the land, growing fruit and vegetables." It was Alexa speaking up, and Annie sensed an immediate atmosphere of surprise, as if the family was unused to the child making a voluntary contribution to the general conversation.

"That must be jolly hard work." Annie smiled back at him, thinking that his restrained manner was very different from his more extrovert brother. Then she turned back towards Alexa, wondering how to encourage the little girl to keep talking, but hardly knowing what to say that might interest her. It was a surprise, then, to hear Alexa herself plunge into more chatter.

"If I ask him he will give you something to take home, won't you, Spyro?"

The boy nodded, his lean face filling with warmth as he smiled at his little niece. Annie realised, with a stab of pleasure, that Alexa was truly loved; the thought gave her considerable joy. Then there was a footstep outside in the court-yard, a diminishing of the sun that poured through the open doorway and Annie looked up into the heart-shaped, vital face of the girl who stood there.

"Katnina, you're late." Marcus smiled down the table, very much the patriarch of his family. "Sit down - beside Annie. Annie, this is Katnina."

Annie nodded, unable to find words that would establish an ordinary, everyday relationship between herself and the beautiful Greek girl. For this was David's Katnina, clearly recognisable from the huge portrait in the cabin on the headland. David's Katnina, whom he surely loved, who had shared that flamboyant couch where she herself had, briefly, lain, where

David's light kisses had sent tingles running down her spine . . .

Katnina slipped into her place, smiling sidewards. "Ah yes, Annie, Alexa has told me about you. You've come to clear up poor Marcus's muddles, yes?" Her husky voice was still, without any sort of emotion, although Annie felt a quick pinprick of tension in the air.

"Well, I suppose you might say that."

"We all know what a muddler, a schemer, Marcus is." Katnina's face flicked a brief smile at him. "But we love him, in spite of it."

"Yes, of course." Annie was fascinated by the girl beside her. Such fluent, easy English—and the luscious figure held the same sort of magnetism that David's powerful personality did. All too well could she see them together, complementing each other, smiling with the same kind of subtle attraction.

Across the table Marcus's eyes recalled her wandering attention.

"Katnina is getting betrothed very soon," he said impishly, and at once his sister shook her head at him, the colour leaving her cheeks for a moment. "How can you say that?" she muttered. "He hasn't asked me yet . . ."

Marcus grinned back at her. "He will, he will! Who could resist you, little sister, once you've made up that resolute mind? Oh yes, we'll have a betrothal party soon and then a marriage, and then—"

"Stop it, Marcus. You're embarrassing us all." But Katnina didn't really look embarrassed, thought Annie shrewdly— she seemed tense and unhappy, even unsure about her future.

"Where is David today?" Unknowingly, Georgious hit the nail on the head and Annie's smile faded, as ripples of uneasy emotion began to ferment inside her.

"Away on business." Marcus's reply was quick and smooth, and he changed the subject at once. "Now, we must arrange about taking Alexa to the hospital tomorrow, for the plaster to be removed. I'll take her down in the car and leave her there—Katnina, you'll come too and bring her home, won't you? I have much to do tomorrow . . ."

"Perhaps I can help?" Annie asked impulsively and then stopped as Katnina's deep eyes fixed on her own.

"That is most kind. But the family looks after Alexa. We know you have much work to do, too, so don't worry, please. The day is my own—I work in the evenings, you see."

Annie nodded and was thankful to hear the voices mixing in a more general discussion of how best to arrange tomorrow's events.

When the meal was over and tiny cups of thick, sweet Turkish coffee were handed around, she watched the boys go outside with polite, smiling apologies towards her. Marcus's mother wheeled Alexa into the adjoining room—"for a siesta," said Marcus quietly, watching his daughter disappear—and Katnina busied herself in washing the dirty dishes. Annie made a move to help, but Marcus shook his head.

"No, no, you're a visitor. Come out and sit in the shade—there's a comfy chair in the yard."

"Shouldn't we be getting back soon?"

"Plenty of time. No one works in the heat of the afternoon. That's right, Annie —relax. Excuse me now, I must talk to Katnina."

Alone in the shaded courtyard, with bougainvillaea blooming in a purple mass as it swept down the wall behind her, it was heaven to close her eyes for a few minutes and think quietly over the emotions and thoughts that the conversation at dinner-time had produced. So Katnina was in love with David—obvious, wasn't it?—even though she didn't want the fact broadcast. Maybe he hadn't popped the question yet. Annie sighed. But of course, he soon would. They were old friends, almost brought up together, as Marcus had told her. And then there was the tell-tale portrait in David's cabin; what could be more implicit than that?

In spite of the sun's heat, Annie felt suddenly chill. Opening her eyes, she stared around the yard, without seeing the brilliance of the flowering plants, the fresh, sweet greenery of the vines that threaded across the space between wall and roof-edge; all she could see in that moment was David's face, his handsome, querulous smile, and the expression of gentleness in his eyes when he had found her on the couch in the cabin. Again, as in a dream, she heard the intimate murmur of his low voice, so close to her.

She jerked to her feet, stepped across the yard with a sort of desperation and met Marcus in the doorway.

"Can we go now? I feel guilty about not working—I'd like to get back to the villa as soon as we can."

"But—"

"Please Marcus."

He shrugged, then called back into the cottage. "Mama, we are leaving now."

His mother's kindly smile relaxed some of Annie's tension. "You will come again, *Thespinis?* You will always be welcome here."

"You've been so kind, I'd love to come again—and thank you for the excellent meal. Goodbye, now."

Katnina appeared in the doorway, waving a casual hand, and the boys' heads poked up over the far wall. "Goodbye, Annie."

"Come again, Annie."

The mule jolted down the hillside, each jerk of its legs making Annie rock on the hard saddle, but she didn't feel the discomfort. Her mind was elsewhere. And even Marcus's warm and friendly presence at the animal's head did nothing to dispel the deep unhappiness that seemed abruptly to have frozen her foolish heart.

4

SLOWLY, though, she returned to reality, caught up in Marcus's unceasing chatter.

"Alexa enjoyed being with you." Clearly, he was speaking his thoughts aloud. With an effort she refocussed her mind.

"She's a super child, Marcus."

"Yes, a sweet nature, just like her mother. My poor Ourania."

"Alexa must miss her very much . . ."

"We both do, Annie."

"Of course. But you're an adult, you've got other interests—other loves, maybe?"

"No, no, I can love only Ourania for ever."

Annie's mind was still bewildered at all she had seen and heard, the different impressions blinding her to the fact that she might be speaking of things that were none of her business. "Haven't you thought of marrying again, though? Alexa needs a mother's love."

"One day, maybe—when I find the right woman." He turned, his pale eyes flashing in the sunlight, and his smile sweeping over her face. In her ear a warning voice whispered; she returned the smile as impersonally as possible and changed the subject.

"You live in a very lovely place—I hope you appreciate how lucky you are."

The image of his mother's veined hands and stooping back brought a quick frown to her face, making her add at once, "But, as you say, it would be a hard life for you all without the holiday trade."

"It puts the jam on our bread. Otherwise, yes, we are poor. No money for dealing with the unexpected things that fate brings."

"Accidents?" Annie picked up his thoughts immediately.

He nodded, the smile quite vanished. "Earthquakes, hospitals, operations, special food, taxis . . ." His broad shoulders shrugged descriptively.

"But you have a good job, Marcus, so you've been able to make out all right." She hoped that he wouldn't think she was being too curious—suspicious, even.

"Oh, yes!" There was a sardonic note in the words that made her look at him sharply, but he had turned away and was pointing ahead, to a breathtaking view of the glimmering, sunlit sea. "Nearly back now. You can have a rest, and then we'll see what messages Anthula has taken."

Annie's head had begun to ache, just a slight niggle over the eyes and her whole body hurt as she swayed in time with the jolting mule, feeling the cumbersome pressure of the hard saddle on her muscles. Now that they were leaving the shelter of the full-foliaged trees, the afternoon sun poured down mercilessly. How good it was to get down from her uncomfortable perch at last when they reached the shabby cottage and its smiling owner. He sat patiently by the open door, hat falling forward over his handsome nose like a poor man's Clint Eastwood, thought Annie, with an abrupt resurge of her never-failing sense of humour.

Resonant Greek chatter erupted around her, with much rolling of R's and easy laughter, but she was feeling increasingly limp and only ready for the cool solitude of her bedroom in the usual afternoon siesta. So it was with a bad attack of returning guilt that she saw the blue car once more parked outside the villa. David had come back unexpectedly—what on earth would he say, finding his staff away and the office unmanned?

Her heart fell into panicky confusion for a moment and then her quick temper flared, pulling up with it her natural fighting spirit. All right, if David wanted a battle then she would give back as good as she received . . .

But it was going to be hard on poor Marcus, already in trouble with his boss and now likely to become even more deeply embroiled. And in a way, Annie felt, much against her will, that she was responsible for Marcus taking the morning off; the whole episode was really her fault.

They approached the villa somewhat sheepishly, silent and aware of their joint irresponsibility. David was sitting at the office desk, deep in contemplation of a list of scribbled messages. He eyed them coldly as they came to a halt in the doorway, standing there waiting for the sword to fall.

"Ah, the runaways returned. How good

of you to come back. Perhaps you even intend to do a little work?" The ice in his words was unpleasantly emphasised by his frozen stare. Before they could answer he abruptly rasped back the chair and got to his feet, scowling across the room, words tumbling out in a tirade that made both Annie and Marcus bow their heads, as the truth of what he said impressed itself on them.

"You're a couple of useless malingerers! How can I hope to run a competent business without any staff? If it wasn't for Anthula taking messages the Villa Estate office would have been completely deserted today; as it is, her writing's so bad and her English so hopeless that I can't understand half of what she's written."

Marcus stepped up to the desk. "Let me deal with them—"

"Oh yes, all of a sudden you're extremely business-like and responsible, but if I hadn't come back unexpectedly like this I daresay you'd still be out somewhere enjoying yourselves; no doubt seeing the car here again jolted your consciences. Marcus, you've let me down, damn you, and it's not the first time."

Marcus grinned awkwardly and tried to charm his way out of the situation. "No, no, you're wrong, David. What are a few messages, after all? Everything will be all right—I'll deal with them at once . . ."

"It certainly isn't all right, don't fool yourself! Why do you suppose I'm back so early? Because the audit proved so complex that the accountants phoned the airport to catch me before I left—they haven't been able to fathom things out yet, and they reckon it'll take at least three more days for them to do so." David turned away from Marcus with irritation all over his face, steely eyes falling at once on Annie. "And as for *you*, my dear Miss Frayne, I suppose you think this is nothing more than a free-for-all holiday?" He paused, took a deep breath, then returned to the attack with renewed force, as if her silence infuriated him further. "The minute my back's turned, off you go with our persuasive friend here—well, I'm disappointed, Annie; I expected better of you."

Her pent-up anger exploded uncontrollably. Wild words came out with a spitting sense of self-righteous justification.

"Expected better? Oh, but you didn't Mr. Nicholas—not really, did you? Ever since we first met you've done nothing but insinuate what a useless, irresponsible creature I am. Do you know, I think you're actually quite pleased to find that your first impressions of me were right? Except that they're *not*. Let me tell you, I worked long hours yesterday without any let-up, and although I agree that Marcus and I should never have left the office unmanned, we did call on all the villa owners early this morning—and we had every intention of working through the evening to make up for the time we'd lost. So just think about that, Mr. Nicolas, and don't be in such a hurry, in future, to accuse your staff, when you don't know the true facts of the case!"

"My God—what a little hellcat!" He glared back at her, eyes narrowed into obvious dislike, clearly taken aback by her impetuous outburst.

Oh, the glorious freedom of such uninhibited expression! Annie's guilt had long since disappeared, and now she felt herself glowing with enjoyment. She returned his stare with equal venom and rallied her forces for a last attack. "Not quite the little mouse you once thought me?" she taunted, and had the satisfaction of seeing the colour rush through his cheeks as the barb went home.

Suddenly her eye caught the expression on Marcus's watching face as he stood beside David, the pile of queries in his hands. He was smiling, nodding his head, as if encouraging her to continue; the fire inside her was quenched as if by a bucket of water—what had she said? What harm had she done? No doubt she really had put her foot in it, adding tinder to a slow fire that had already been kindled between the two men because of Marcus's incompetency. How awful of her to side with Marcus, when she knew only too well that he was clearly in the wrong . . .

The triumph slid away; a vague dizziness made her head swim abruptly, and she staggered, reaching out a hand to grasp the nearest chair. But it was a human support that she encountered—a cool, masculine hand bearing her up and, with the addition of a strong arm around her waist, leading her out of the office, down the passage and into her own bedroom.

The welcome quietness and shade of the shuttered room revived her at once, even though David's presence was tormenting and unwanted.

"You've had too much sun. Lie down —no, don't talk." His voice was unexpectedly gentle all of a sudden. Her shoes were slipped off and her wobbly legs lifted on to the bed. She feigned further weakness to give herself time to sort out the impossible situation.

She knew now that she had been irresponsible and rude; and he was being so kind and understanding—but how much easier it would be if he was still shouting at her . . .

Through her lashes she dared to glance up. He stood above her, a tall, fearsome figure of powerful dominance; but, to her extreme surprise, he was smiling, a wry sort of smile that suggested he was the type of man who appreciated courage in a worthy adversary. A man, perhaps, who bore no malice, once the fight was done.

Annie allowed herself to stare openly at him. "I'm not going to say I'm sorry," she muttered, trying defiantly to sit up, because it was disconcerting to remain so far below him, but he merely put a hand on her shoulder, pushing her down again, his mouth lifting in a reluctant grin.

"I don't expect you to. Not yet, anyway. You're in such a state you can't think straight."

Such patronising ideas made her blink. Shrugging away his hand she struggled anew, finally sitting up and leaning against the cane bedhead, breath a little uneven and eyes filled with the last traces of her spent anger.

"I'm—I'm *not* in a state . . ."

He left her then, stalking across to the window where he opened the shutters, turned and leaned out against the balcony wall, finally looking back with a mocking expression that enraged her still further. "Of course you are. It's all been too much for you—the journey here, the sun, Marcus and his charm, the emotions you've doubtless been pouring all over that child of his . . . I think you need a good long rest to get over it. Stay in bed, my dear Miss Frayne; get some sleep. *And sort yourself out!*" The last infuriating remark was made as he strode past her and out of the door.

"I'll do no such thing!" Her shrill voice was a pitiful, useless protest. The door slammed and, with disbelief, she heard the key being turned. Locked in? But it was incredible—

All weakness gone, she leaped off the bed and raced to the window, standing irresolute as she realised that escape this way was impossible, the villa being built into the hillside and resting on supports some twelve feet off the ground.

She was a prisoner. Annie returned to the bed and sat down, thinking hard, conflicting thoughts circling her aching head. What a beast he was—how dare he treat her like this? She would get out somehow, she would tell the world what a monster David Nicholas was, she would let Marcus console her, she would . . .

"I'll leave you to clear up things then, Marcus. My turn to have some time off, I think. I'm going down to the cabin."

David's clear voice at the far end of the villa was imperative and unconcerned. It filled her with a kind of anguish, so hard to understand that she grew cross with herself. She *must* hate him, really she must; he had treated her abominably, so why this ridiculous urge to forgive and forget?

From the side of the little balcony she watched his tall figure—divested now of the elegant business suit, clad only in frayed jeans with a navy shirt dangling over tanned shoulders, above which the sun-touched hair gleamed and shone—walk briskly down the hillside towards the headland path, disappearing into the green blur of the pines even as her eyes yearned over him.

And then, as she turned away miserably, deciding against her will to take his advice and get some sleep, a flash of coloured movement caught her flagging attention. Someone else was going into the pine-woods, dressed in a bright skirt that she had seen very recently, a girl with dark hair and a glorious figure . . . Katnina, of course. Going to meet David in the cabin, thought Annie, imagination suddenly unhappily inspired; going to share a siesta in the cool shade of the trees, with the sea whispering a love song in the cove below, and the comfort of that flamboyant couch inducing in them both a languid passion that Annie couldn't bear to think about.

She tossed on her modestly narrow bed and at last allowed the traitorous tears of frustration and remorse to spill out, unheeded, all over her pillow. She wished she had never come to Doloffinos, never met the arrogant, uncaring and quite maddeningly attractive David Nicholas.

Eventually she slept; the darkening evening found the door still locked, but a tray of supper put by her bedside before she awoke. Headache gone, Annie found it easier to think. Anger and a painful awareness of her own childishness gave way at last as the pangs of every-day hunger took over. Sitting on the balcony, meditating in the silence of the sunset, Annie discovered that her sense of humour was slowly returning. Imprisoned? Rather the punishment usually meted out to a naughty child . . . gradually she began to smile and to reluctantly admit that David had done no more than she deserved. She might even find it in her heart to forgive him—but then the smile faded. For she knew it wouldn't matter a jot to him what she did—he had Katnina, and no need of a simple, naive English secretary with a quick temper.

Surprisingly, she slept well that night, awaking to the morning sun with a pleasant sense of well-being. She wondered if her subconscious had perhaps sorted out a few of the more pressing conflicts while she slept and then smiled, her irrepressible mind visualising David's contemptuous put-down, should she ever dare to suggest such an unacceptable notion to him. Because, of course, any fancy ideas like that would be far removed from his starkly physical, materialistic mind; then abruptly, as she dressed, she recalled the atmospheric quality of some of the paintings she had seen in the cabin, and wondered anew.

Opening the shutters to let in the fresh light, Annie looked at the evocative landscape with a tight feeling in her throat. Such beauty! Already she knew she loved the island and felt at home there. Then she corrected herself edgily; she was a visiting foreigner and nothing more. Britain, with its more casual beauty, was her home-ground, and she would do well to remember the fact.

And yet . . . briefly she sighed for something she couldn't understand, that was making unfamiliar demands in her usually disciplined, ordinary life, and felt the underlying emotions surge to the surface as the wind touched the pine trees on the headland, caressing their dark caps and drawing from them the sensuous music that she would always remember, even when her visit to Doloffinos was just a dream of the past; when she was back in the London office, drinking coffee with Sandra and dealing with Eric's calculating hiccups.

Then, once more, David Nicholas would be just a name printed on the firm's letter-heading, the boss's son who dealt with problems in faraway places, and who never even recognised her in the rare event of their passing on a crowded corridor.

Annie's head lifted resolutely as she brushed her hair. She must be sensible and think of the future, not of the disturbing effect which this languorous and beautiful place was having on her stupidly romantic dreams. She had a good job with much potential and she would return to it, forgetting the madness of her fantasies about David. And if she wanted to keep her job—upon which all her future happiness was based—then she must cast his magnetic attraction out of her mind and apply herself to the work that awaited in the office. She must, also, apologise to him . . .

That decided, there was only one thing to do. Without further thought, she finished dressing, took out her writing case, sat on the bed and chewed her pen.

"Dear Mr. Nicholas." So far, so good. The next bit was more difficult. "I apologise—" Inside her a slight rumble of defiance briefly remonstrated, but she quelled it and wrote on steadily, ". . . for my bad behaviour and lack of responsibility. I hope you will allow me to return to work and finish the job for which you brought me here. I undertake to give you no further problems."

She re-read the note and sighed before signing her name.

Annie Frayne.

There, it was done, a bitter defeat, but a lesson well learned. Perhaps in future she would now be better able to curb that wretchedly quick temper before it landed her in fresh trouble.

She addressed the note to David, then pushed it beneath the locked door before she could change her mind. Then there was nothing to do but wait for her jailer-and-judge to reconsider his verdict, so she started a long letter to her family.

"It's really lovely here," she scribbled, "and the island people very friendly." That made her think of Marcus and the fact that Alexa was to have her plaster removed today. Then came the thought that she would dearly like to visit the child later in the day, to see how she was, to find out if the fracture was at last healing, to see the thin face smiling again, now that freedom was in sight. But if she wanted to take time off, she would have to ask permission of David. That is, she told herself gloomily, if he ever comes near me again . . .

She cocked her head; did she hear footsteps outside the door? Holding her breath she waited for the possible turn of the key, for that unmistakable, vibrant voice either berating her further, or even kindly enquiring how she had slept . . . he was so unpredictable that either course of action was possible. But no, nothing happened. Maybe it was just Anthula who had found the envelope and borne it away, to be read later when the big boss felt so inclined.

Annie fidgetted; how long did he intend to keep her here, for heaven's sake? She applied herself to her letter home, quickly becoming immersed in what she was writing. There was so much to tell them —nothing, of course, about David—but a full description of her visit to Marcus's home, little bits about Spyro and his vegetables, about Georgious's passion for football, Mama's fish dinner and Alexa's poor leg.

The door was unlocked and opened without her realising it. Anthula came in, bearing a freshly laden breakfast tray. She said pleasantly, *"Kalimera*, Annie. I hope you sleep well?"

"Yes, thanks, Anthula." Annie's glance fell on the stiff white envelope resting against the silver-plated coffee pot. "Is that for me?" she asked foolishly.

"From David. He went out for a sail

directly after breakfast. Is there anything else, Annie?"

"No thanks, this is fine."

Anthula left and Annie listened tensely for the key to grate but the door remained unlocked. So the prisoner had been freed . . . she ripped open the envelope and took the briefly written note out onto the little balcony. The heavy writing bore the impact of David's strong personality and a tingle ran through her as she read, almost hearing the usual wry mockery in his deep voice.

"My dear Miss Frayne—or may I call you Annie? Your apology is accepted. I suggest we both forget what we said to each other in the heat of the moment yesterday. The work of clearing the accounts and re-organising the running of the villas is all-important, and we would both do well to remember the fact. Please continue with the work, on which I acknowledge you have already made a substantial start.

Yours, David.

For a moment quick irritation possessed

her—how typical of him to be so bossy and patronising! *Your apology* is *accepted*, indeed. She crumpled the paper in a spontaneous gesture of annoyance and was about to send it flying over the balcony, when something stopped her. Recalling the next sentence, she slowly straightened out the paper, realising that a certain humility was present in the uncompromising words—*we would both do well to remember the fact.* He was right, of course, the work was the only truly important factor of the situation, and it was honest of him to admit it. Personal feelings didn't enter into it at all.

Maybe he wasn't so devastatingly arrogant as he had at first appeared; maybe he, like everybody else in the world, put a face on things and hid behind it; maybe . . . thoughtfully, Annie folded the note and put it in her bag before she sat in the sun and ate her solitary breakfast, eyes fixed on the stretching, hazy sea where, somewhere out of sight, David's boat would be dipping and swerving like a bird in flight.

The office was empty when she entered it, but she had already heard Marcus arrive and leave again, his cheerful voice echoing through the villa.

"Anthula! I'm taking Alexa to the hospital—I'll be back mid-morning. Annie will look after things till then."

She thought of calling out to him, but decided not to. He had enough on his mind today. So she applied herself to the work that waited, and suddenly it was nearly noon when she finally looked up from the heavy ledger and the adjacent calculator. Her mind buzzed alarmingly. She didn't like what she was discovering —so many discrepancies that surely couldn't all be dismissed as careless writing. It was beginning to mount up to one, unbelievable fact—that Marcus was quite cheerfully cheating his employers.

Annie got up and strolled out onto the terrace for a minute's respite. She needed fresh air and a change of scene; the sun was ferociously hot and she stood in the shade of the huge oleander bush that grew just beyond the terrace wall.

Behind her the villa lay empty and quiet, Anthula having prepared the cold lunch and then gone home. Presumably

David was still sailing and Marcus hadn't yet returned.

Her thoughts were restless and confused again. There was so much happening here that it was difficult to know what to concentrate on next. The shock about Marcus's accounts gave way reluctantly to the image of Alexa, pale-faced and nervous as Annie had first seen her, with the long, brilliantly white plaster-cast stretched in front of her. Was the child still at the hospital? Had the doctor discovered that the break was healing at long last?

Annie shook her head, distressed at her own lack of control. She was becoming too emotional, just as David had predicted. It was foolish to worry about things that she couldn't change; and yet . . .

When footsteps sounded in the hallway she turned, half-smiling in anticipation of seeing Marcus, and perhaps Alexa, too, but it was David who came into view and halted abruptly when he saw her on the terrace.

"Oh!" she said, nonplussed, feeling her cheeks flame. "I thought you were Marcus; I mean—I didn't know . . ."

"Marcus is catching up on yesterday's

chores—I hope." David's tone was dry, and he did no more than give her a quick glance as he joined her on the terrace.

"Yes, of course." She swallowed the lump in her throat and felt stupidly uncomfortable. For a long moment there was silence.

Then—"I wonder if . . ." she began, at the same time as David turned and said, "How about a drink before lunch?"

Their eyes met and the awkward moment dissolved as slowly they smiled, releasing the tension that had grown between them.

"Sit down and relax," David ordered lightly as he went back into the villa. "Go on—do as you're told. I don't want any more trouble from you, Annie Frayne."

He came out with glasses of limonada and pulled his chair over to sit beside her, with a small table between them. "Right now, let's get things straight, shall we? You apologised, I accepted your apology, and so we can make a new start. Agreed?"

With a struggle she pulled her gaze away from his vividly coloured eyes and looked demurely down at her drink. "Agreed, Mr. Nicholas."

"David."

Something in his voice made her look up. "Of course—David."

Their eyes clung unexpectedly and she sought for words that would restore their relationship to that of boss and employee. "The ledgers . . ." She clutched at the first diversion that came into her churning mind. "The ledgers are nearly up to date, but I'm finding more and more discrepancies, I'm afraid. It looks as if—" She bit her lip, unable to be the one to accuse Marcus, but David finished the sentence for her, his voice impersonal and casual.

". . . as if our Greek friend has been doing a nice little job of feathering his own nest at our expense. Yes, it certainly looks that way."

"But why?" Now the matter was in the open, she was unable to keep her curiosity at bay. "I mean, he has a good job, so why should he have to—to—"

"Steal? I can't imagine. But I intend to find out." David's face was suddenly sombre. "At one time Marcus and I were able to talk straight to each other; but things are different now, somehow. We're at cross purposes, and I don't know why."

Annie was aghast at such revelations. Shyly, she said, "Hasn't it struck you that there must be a reason for what he's done? I mean, you know Marcus very well, don't you?"

"I thought I knew him." David's voice was low and bitter and Annie's eyes widened. She could hardly believe the fact that he was opening up like this; here was no mere boss whose right-hand man had been found cheating; no, he was a human being, betrayed by a friend of long-standing, and clearly finding the experience painful.

"Of course, you're blood-brothers . . ." She spoke without thought, and he lifted his head immediately, staring hard at her.

"What do you know about that?"

"I'm sorry, it's none of my business—but Marcus told me . . ."

"Dear God, so he can tell our secrets to a stranger and yet push me out into the cold like this." David flung out of the chair to pace up and down the terrace, his face hard and set.

Annie's heart pounded, but she said determinedly, "Perhaps he just hasn't had a chance to tell you—"

"Damn it, whose side are you on?" David's anger flared quickly. "You're working for my father—for *me*, in fact—so why find excuses for Marcus?" His eyes dwelt on her for a long moment and then he smiled unpleasantly. "But then, I suppose Marcus's easy charm has very soon made a friend of you—I'd forgotten for the minute all about the pretty British girls and their appeal for the skirt-chasing local lads . . ."

"That's beastly and quite uncalled for," Annie answered sharply, her sympathy abruptly dispelled. "And what's more, it's totally untrue. Marcus has been friendly, certainly—he's that sort of man—"

"Only too well do I know the sort of man he is." David laughed challengingly. "Don't tell me he hasn't kissed you yet!" Halting in his pacing, he flashed a searching glance at her, and her anger subsided like a pricked balloon. She felt the traitorous colour surge into her cheeks.

"That's no business of yours!"

"And that's no answer. But your face tells me the truth—of course he's kissed you—made love to you, perhaps? Out there, on the moonlit beach? On the mountainside, under those conveniently concealing evergreens? After all, who can resist a holiday romance? Well, I'm surprised at you, Annie Frayne—you told me you don't play that sort of game, but it seems that you're keeping your options open. Makes me wonder what Marcus has got that I don't have."

They stared at each other, tempers fanned to a fighting pitch. And then, as if they shared their thoughts, both spoke together.

"I'm sorry Annie . . . forgive me, that's an outrageous thing to say to you . . ."

"Don't let's fight, David."

The sun shone onto the terrace and the wind hummed through the pines and suddenly the awful moment was over. Shame-faced, David said gently, "We've just got time for a bit of a blow out in the boat; help us to cool down, maybe. Say you'll come, Annie?"

She hesitated, wondering yet again at the quicksilver changes of mood that flickered through this man. Then she saw the pleading in his eyes and perceived a humility that hadn't been apparent before.

"I'd love to come."

Their smiles linked and she felt a glow rising through her. With it came the reminder that she badly needed to ask a favour of him—quickly she took advantage of his good humour, and said, "But before we go, may I ask if I could have a couple of hours off to go and see Alexa this afternoon? I'll willingly make up the time—you see, she had her plaster off this morning and I said I would visit her, if possible . . ."

David stood, looking down at her, his face full of a new understanding, his voice quiet as he answered, "Tell you what, I'll take you up to the cottage after you've had your siesta. We'll pack up our lunch now and have it on the boat after a swim. You've worked hard this morning, the breeze out there will do you good. So come on, up you get . . ."

It was with a sense of living in a dream-world that she obeyed, following him into the kitchen and helping to pack the salad and the cheese, with accompanying loaves and butter, into a basket covered with a teatowel; watching while he found glasses and a bottle of wine and a corkscrew, then treading in his footsteps as they went down the hot, dusty path, into the shade of the singing pines and finally climbing into the dinghy that lay side up on the clean sand of the cove below.

Even the thought of Katnina, whose portrait hung in the cabin, and whose watching presence must even now be frowning upon her, did nothing to prevent Annie's joy from bubbling up and overflowing.

As the outboard motor roared into life and the dinghy chugged out to the slender yacht that danced on its mooring in the neck of the headland, she smiled into David's face, and was entranced to see that the smile he returned was as carefree as her own.

5

"**N**ECK and neck!"

"No, I was an inch ahead . . ."

Annie watched David pull his dripping body over the side of the boat, and then allowed him to help her aboard.

They were both breathing fast after their swim, hair slickly outlining their laughing faces. David found a towel in the stern and threw it down on the hot boards. "You can dry off there and I'll get a drink. Must be mad, all this exercise in the middle of the day."

Minutes later he put a long glass of iced liquid beside her, and sat on a gunwhale a few yards away. She shaded her eyes from the glare of the overhead sun, and watched him take a long drink before he ran tanned fingers through the mop of silver hair, now dulled to a pewter greyness by the water. He made a striking figure, she thought, so tall and lean and handsome. Even his stillness was dynamic. She couldn't take her eyes off him.

He caught her in mid-stare. "Penny for them."

"Oh!" Flustered, she sat up to drink and tried to change the subject. "Mmmmm, real lemonade; gorgeous."

"Don't prevaricate, Annie. Answer the question."

"I don't really know what I was thinking . . ." She kept her face down.

"You're a rotten liar," observed David wryly. "If you want people to believe them when you tell untruths you must act it out, you know—face them, smile a little— don't look as if you were ashamed of yourself."

That brought her head up with a jerk. "I'm not ashamed!" So the old anger was still there, she thought ruefully, and smiled at him, trying to keep it in check.

"So—if you're not ashamed, you can tell me what you were thinking."

"Well . . ."

In one quick, lithe movement he was beside her, body flopping down on the deck, his glass placed carefully next to hers. He turned on his side, leaning on one bronzed arm, . and regarded her surprised face thoughtfully.

"You've got freckles, Annie Frayne. Quite a lot of them. Sun-kisses."

Annie edged away uneasily. He was at it again, playing games, just as he had done on the night of their arrival. Hoping that he wouldn't notice her alarm, she said airily, "When I was a little girl I used to get up at dawn and go out and rub dew on them to make them go."

He raised one bleached eyebrow, "What on earth for?"

"It's an old country custom."

"I know that. I meant, why did you want to get rid of them?"

"Because they're—they're blemishes . . ." She was wretchedly aware of his closeness.

"Ridiculous. They're beautiful. Pretty little round golden-brown sun-kisses. You've got them on your nose, and your forehead, and—" Leaning even closer, his face was only an inch away from hers.

Annie gasped and murmured helplessly, feeling like a hypnotised rabbit about to be grabbed by a murderous stoat. ". . . and . . . and. . . ?"

"Around your lips." He made no further move, but simply stared at her mouth, while it half-opened in surprise and fright, and then shut again very swiftly, clamping itself into a thin, defensive line. Reacting quickly, she got up, and perched on a narrow plank a safe distance from him; without comment he, too, rose and went to the cabin where the luncheon basket was stowed. Coming back he slid down to the boards again, fishing out the wine and the glasses and pushing the basket towards her.

"Get the salad together while I do this . . ."

She put a loaded plate near him and took the wine he offered. About to sip, she was pulled gently but firmly off her seat and down to the bottom of the board beside him. His arm pulled a weathered canvas bollard towards her.

"Lean against this—that's right. Come on, relax, girl, you can't be all prim and proper in the middle of the Aegean, you know—"

He was right, of course. He always was. It was wonderful down there in the well of the boat, hearing the water lapping at ear-level, feeling part of the element and not just a visitor, at odds with it.

Annie felt the hot boards beneath her bare legs as she sipped the wine. It was cool and fruity, suggesting leafy groves and rich, sensual crops of smooth velvet . . . unthinkingly she let her warm fingers stroke the white pillar of her throat as the liquid trickled down, satiating her taste-buds, provocative and dangerous. Then she laid her head back against the hard pillow of the bollard. Salt smells, exotic tastes, the music of the sea—all such sensuous, beautiful things . . . with a huge effort she put down the wine glass and looked at the plate on her lap. She must keep a firm control of herself. It was all getting rather too much, being out here on the water, with David so near to her.

Once the plates were emptied he refilled their glasses, even though she refused her share. "No, thank you," she said, but he went on pouring, laughing at her quietly until she realised how unnecessarily old-fashioned she was being. Against all her inclinations, she found herself joining in with his infectious mirth.

What a fool she was, a cold English miss, who was afraid to let go and learn just what life had to offer, here in this enchanted lotus-eating land. As if he read her thoughts, David's laughter died. He stared curiously at her, letting his eyes wander down over her body, from her reddening cheeks to the tense tips of her bare toes.

Then—"Annie," he said at last, his voice quiet as if talking to a child, warmly tinged with humour and patience, "Annie, isn't it time you grew up? You can't stay a child for ever, you know . . ."

For a moment she couldn't answer. He was right, so right—but this was hardly the moment to agree, out here alone in the boat with him, with the wind whispering mischievous thoughts and the sea singing a love song that was as old as time.

Oh yes, the temptation was there, and inside her the urge to give in to it was growing irresistibly stronger, minute by minute. But there was—Katnina. Thankfully, Annie held on to the name as it flashed through her churning mind. David had Katnina to love, he didn't need her as well. She wouldn't be a party to the games he played; *she wouldn't.*

She sat up straighter, shaking back the hair that blew about her hot face. Avoiding the impelling gaze that seemed to read every emotion that swept through her, she said stiffly, "I'll grow up when I'm good and ready, and not before. I like being young and—and—"

The missing word formed on her lips, but she couldn't get it out. Instead, she blushed rosily and wished she was dead. David's green eyes never left her face as he supplied it for her. "—and innocent. That's what you were going to say, Annie, weren't you?"

"Y—yes." Wretchedly, she stared back at him, aghast at the feelings that pounded inside her.

"So be it." He sighed, then rolled away from her, rising to his feet and repacking the luncheon basket. "And who am I to force you to change your mind? Don't tell me—" as she opened her mouth to demur, "—your boss, that's who. Hardly the one to dictate the development of your private life." His voiced changed abruptly. "We'd better get back, the wind's changing. We'll have to do a quick run . . ."

Minutes later he called to her from the stern, where he sat with the rudder by his right hand. "Come here, Annie."

She thought she had never seen him so relaxed and happy. Attractive, too. Shyly she shook her head. He was too unpredictable, too charismatic. She couldn't cope with any more games . . .

"Please, Annie."

Slowly, wondering at her lack of self-discipline, and yet at the same time aware of pleasure surging within her, she went to his side.

"You can steer." He pulled her down beside him, so close that the warmth of his body added another dimension to her sharp enjoyment.

"But I don't know how . . ."

"It's easy. Like this."

His sure hand guided hers for a little while, and soon her confidence grew. "I can do it myself now." There was a special sort of joy in controlling the leaping, fragile craft, she discovered. The sea whispered and the mounting wind sang in the rigging as the boat flew before it. Annie threw back her head and let the sun caress her freckled cheeks. The moment was sheer heaven and she never wanted it to stop. But all too soon David's hand took possession once more of the rudder and his voice at her ear said firmly, "I'll take over here . . ."

He nodded ahead, to where a froth of breaking waves crowned a small black toothy ridge of rock. "It's called the Black Handkerchief—well, go on, ask me why . . ."

Enjoying the expression of concentration on his face, admiring the professional ease with which he steered the boat past the danger point, even as she shivered at the incipient menace of the seemingly innocent-looking rock, she said obediently, "All right; why?"

"There's a local folk story of how a young boy was drowned here, crashing his fishing boat on the rock. His mother came out at low tide afterwards to mourn him, and stayed, even as the water began to rise again. You know how all the village matrons cover their hair with dark scarves? Well, when the tide went out again all that was left of this particular woman was her black handkerchief. Hence the name." He glanced back over his shoulder. "Safe again. You can take over now, if you like."

It was like riding a horse, she decided, her satisfaction returning as she handled the leaping boat. Up and down in a joyous ryhthm, with enough hidden sense of danger to keep the concentration steady and focussed. When David again took the rudder from her, the disappointment must have showed on her face, for he said encouragingly, "You've done very well—we'll come out again. I'll make a sailor of you yet. Now, watch while I take her into the cove . . ."

The small bay opened before them, a wind-sheltered harbour so suddenly hot and still that it was like entering a vacuum as they slipped in, between the rocky headland and the curve of the stretching beach.

Through the sudden lack of wind, Annie heard the familiar music—the song of the pines above. Staring up at the trees she listened acutely, knowing with bitter abruptness, that she would always recall the lovely sound, even when David was just a remembered name and Doloffinos only a haunting memory.

As her feet touched the warm sand again, so her dreams fell to earth. While they had been out in the boat, caught in the spell of the elements, she had been able to forget her troubles, but now they came surging back, and she was grateful, in a gloomy way, when David said impersonally and briskly, crunching up the beach behind her, "I expect you'll want to have a rest before we go and see Alexa. Take an hour, Annie, and put something cooling on that sunburn. It's always dangerous out there on the water, with the salt and the wind—you were lucky not to get more badly burned . . ."

She coloured, reading into his words a double meaning, and was thankful to escape into the quiet privacy of her room, back at the villa. In the shower she looked at her reflection; the salt and sand-covered girl in the wispy bikini, with wet, clinging hair and no make-up to hide the freckles, had gone. *Sun-kisses*, echoed David's lazily teasing voice. She slapped moisturising cream on her face with one wish suddenly foremost in her mind, to hide them for ever, for now she would never be able to think of them again as mere blemishes.

The quiet hour resting alone gave her a chance to think less subjectively about their exchange of words on the boat; now she realised that she had been partly to blame by so willingly agreeing to go out with him. In a way she supposed she had encouraged him, although such a thought had never entered her mind. He was a man of the world and certainly must be used to taking pleasure when and where he wished. What a stupid child he must think her! While innocence was one thing, ignorance of life was quite another. Although she still smarted from the experience, Annie finally accepted that the blame lay with her. Well, she would give him no further opportunities for casual love-making—then it struck her mind with wry certainty that it was unlikely that more invitations would come her way. Why should he bother with her when Katnina, voluptuous and surely more co-operative, was his already?

Annie sighed, as she gave her hair a last brushing. What a good thing she had friends like Alexa and Marcus; she felt she could spend her off-duty time visiting the cottage on the hillside quite happily, as they had asked her to. She need only see David in the office in future.

"Ready, Annie?" His voice intruded

into her busy thoughts as she closed the bedroom door behind her. He stood at the end of the long passage, watching her walk along to join him, keen eyes taking in the glow of her newly acquired sunburn, and the fresh blue and white printed slip of a dress that left her arms bare.

Desperately, she fought for self-control. She would not blush, she would not give him the satisfaction of knowing that his stare upset her . . . "You look gorgeous, Annie—but then, you always do . . ."

Again his unpredictability shattered her, and she followed him out to the car in new confusion.

"Hop in." He was laughing at her, quietly, gently, but with obvious delight. And it was very difficult to keep from smiling back at him.

He chatted casually as they drove up the hillside, telling her that the road was three miles longer than the path which the mules took; that no doubt the trees would soon be chopped down to enable more building plots to be sold, as tourism increased its assault upon the island. Annie merely nodded or shook her head and he didn't seem to expect her to reply. But it did just touch her mind that maybe he was giving her time to recover from his compliment.

At the cottage there was a flurry of movement as the car arrived. Mama stood in the doorway, her face lighting up with a big smile as she recognised the driver.

"Ah, David . . ." She lapsed into her own language and he answered her in Greek, hugging her as he did so. Then he pulled Annie forward.

"And here's Annie . . . she bullied me into bringing her up to see Alexa. Is she back from the hospital? How is she, Mama?"

"See for yourself." Smiling over her shoulder she withdrew inside the cottage.

David nodded at Annie. "In you go."

A small voice shouted her name. "Annie! See, my leg—look, it works!"

Alexa was no longer in her wheelchair. Instead, she sat in the place of honour, the big wooden chair at the head of the table where Marcus had sat yesterday. Crutches were propped up beside her and the unsightly plaster was gone. Helped by her grandmother's careful hands, the child stood up slowly, displaying her uncovered leg for the visitors to inspect.

Annie's heart raced. Such a poor, thin little leg, wasted and frail—would it ever become as thick and strong as its companion? She bent, running her hands lightly down it. "Hallo, leg! It's good to see you again!"

Behind her, David's voice said firmly, "Swimming, Alexa, that's what you need, lots of swimming."

"The doctor said so—it will strengthen the muscles without tiring her." Mama smiled at Alexa and nodded vehemently.

"Easy enough, with the sea at your doorstep. Tell you what, Alexa—" David's voice dropped as he bent down beside her. "I'll teach you to snorkel, how about that? We were talking about it last year, weren't we, before this happened; well, we'll do it now. We'll start tomorrow."

"Oh, David!" Alexa glowed. "Really? Oh, yes please—" Then her face fell. "But with a stiff leg, I can't swim, I shall sink, I . . ."

"Of course you won't sink. We'll take Annie with us, she'll be in charge of your tail while I hold up the front. How about that?"

"Yes; *yes!*"

"That's a date, then. Just before lunch tomorrow—tell Marcus to bring you down first thing and you can sit in the shade while we do some work for a couple of hours. Then we'll all swim."

Alexa began to tell Annie a long tale about how the plaster had been sawn off; and Annie listened with half her mind, wondering about the way David had shown his compassion and his readiness to give his time to the child. Then Mama put glasses of ouzo and a jug of water on the table, and conversation became more general.

"Careful, now," David warned, looking across at Annie with lazy mockery, as he held up the tiny glass. "Plenty of water with it, that's the answer for an innocent girl like you . . ."

She blinked and anger flared, unbidden. So he hadn't forgotten those moments on the boat. Piqued, she stared back at him, and managed to smile sweetly. "Thank you. Your advice is always to the point." Defiantly she drank down the undiluted liquid and immediately felt she was choking to death.

"Poh, poh, poh!" cried Mama, pushing a glass of water towards her.

David patted her back and said firmly, "Don't panic, Annie. Take some deep breaths. Easy does it . . ."

She recovered slowly and then sat limply by Alexa's side, reluctantly grateful to David for engaging the family in earnest Greek conversation. When he finally turned and looked at her, glancing meaningfully at his watch as he did so, she was once again in command of herself.

"I can hear the ledgers calling you home, Annie. Cheerio, Alexa, we'll swim together tomorrow. Good to see you again Mama—my regards to the boys."

Mama's voice called from the cottage doorway as they went towards the car. "And a message for Katnina?"

Annie paused, unable to stop herself looking at David's face. But his reaction was masked. "Not really," he returned smoothly. "I daresay we'll bump into each other some time soon. In you get, Annie . . ."

Friendly farewell waves followed them as they drove back towards the villa, but Annie's astute eyes discerned a certain grimness on Mama's face, beneath the wrinkles and the determined smile.

They were silent, Annie's circling thoughts unable to centre on anything resembling social small-talk; she felt that if she opened her mouth she would ask unforgivable questions. Had he quarrelled with Katnina? Why had Mama gone out of her way to bring up Katnina's name? What was going to happen about Marcus and the accounts . . . ?

David's easy voice returned her to the present. "You're off in that faraway world again," he remarked, grey-green eyes boring into hers for a minute. "Dare I say a penny for them?"

"They're not for sale," she said, knowing her tone was short, but not caring. She realised he knew more about her than she wanted him to know. It put her at a definite disadvantage. But he wouldn't let the subject drop.

"That makes them sound precious," he said mildly. "In which case you must hang on to them. Don't let anyone steal them away."

She stared, amazed at the depth of feeling that had suddenly crept into his voice. Thoughts in her own mind crystallised and she let them tumble out. "Did someone steal *your* precious thoughts once? Is that what you mean?"

He brought the car to a throbbing halt by the side of the road outside the villa, switched off the ignition and turned in his seat so that he looked directly into her surprised face. "Something like that, Annie. And I wouldn't want you to be hurt in the same way. The idealism of youth is very vulnerable. Like I said, guard it well."

Their eyes were caught in a moment of truth; she felt that in those few, quiet words lay the clue to the real David who chose to masquerade beneath a worldly, uncaring facade. And she felt, too, a surge of something approaching uninhibited happiness as she realised that he had confided in her; that, just for this moment, he trusted her, perhaps even valued her friendship.

"David—" His name was pulled from her. His eyes sparked warmly, flickering for a second, as if her soft voice had touched a vital spot.

"I'm sorry about everything ... ." She

longed to let it all flood out; sorry for her quick temper, her rudeness, and the way she had let him down by falling prey to Marcus's persuasiveness; sorry, too, more than anything, for wanting to remain an innocent child and not yet grow into the mature woman he would most definitely prefer.

But, as if he knew that at any moment the dam might overflow, he put a restraining finger against her lips, smiled down into her wide eyes, and said with a quirk of returning humour that was annoying at such a time, yet so desperately attractive, "Not a word more, or you'll say something you regret. Come along, my dear Miss Frayne, what's happened to that tiger-sharp image you cling to so strongly? If you play the mouse for too long, you'll deprive me of my original vision of you . . ."

She wondered, bewildered, just what that original vision might have been, but before she could answer he was out of the car and coming around to her side.

"Back to those damned accounts, Annie. And I've got to take myself in hand

and decide what I'm going to do about the matter."

She followed him into the villa, knowing the sweet and inexplicable moment was over; knowing, too, that it would never return. It was with a very definite lack of concentration that she once again opened the pages of the ledger and stared at the rows of disorderly figures, realising that their disarray concealed a truth that neither she nor David was anxious to find.

"Make us a cup of tea, Annie, there's a love."

She looked up, flustered, torn abruptly from the world of decimal points and profit and loss. *Love?* For a second her heart fluttered; then she accepted it had been just a casual term. He sat there at the opposite side of the room with a frown on his face, oblivious of everything except the papers in front of him. She went and made the tea, returning to put a cup beside him without saying anything.

"Thanks." He lifted his head and stared at the doorway. "This must be Marcus . . ."

The heavy footsteps halted just inside

the office and Annie, after taking one look at the expression on Marcus's face, seeing the easy smile that was suddenly wiped off, leaving a defensive readiness, was alerted to the situation. There was going to be a show-down, she felt it in her knotted stomach, saw all the outward signs of it mounting as the two men faced each other in the hot, airless room.

"Sit down." David was unsmiling, businesslike, his voice crisply concealing what he must be feeling.

Marcus pulled out a chair with swaggering nonchalance, but his intense eyes never left David's face.

"Shall I go?" Annie murmured, already turning towards the door, but knowing instinctively that escape was impossible.

"No. You're in this as much as we are. I'm sorry, Annie, but we've got to face things . . ." David glanced her way and she was surprised that somehow he knew how she was feeling. Stiffly, she returned to her chair and waited for the volcano to erupt.

At first they were both controlled and polite. David said it was clear that Marcus had made false entries over the last few months; could he explain them, please? Marcus, in his turn, smiled charmingly and leaned back in the chair as if he were at home in his own cottage.

"Oh well, a few pounds here and there . . . my writing is bad, I know—"

"It's not just your writing I'm asking about, Marcus—it's your reasoning behind the writing. You're cheating the company, whether it's pounds or thousands. So tell me why."

Marcus's flashing smile slowly faded. He got up, fingers drumming on the back of the chair. "You mean you don't trust me any longer? I'm manager here, remember; I run the place for you. You've always been happy for me to do so—until now. Because that trust is gone, yes?"

David's voice was under tight control. "Stop being so dramatic. You're getting away from the real issue, which isn't trust but money. Come on now, Marcus, explain, for God's sake."

"But how can I explain when you're so cold, so pompous . . . ah David, you've changed, and we can't talk any longer. And it's not my fault."

Annie shivered in the hot room.

Marcus's face was heavy with emotion, his deep voice growing louder and angrier. He leaned across the desk, staring at David. Then his arms suddenly whirled like windmills and he stormed back to the doorway. "I thought you would understand! But here you are, accusing me instead. *Accusing* me!"

The words echoed into a taut silence and David's face never altered. Annie wondered miserably what he was thinking. She longed to run, but was too fascinated to move.

At last he said, reasonably enough, "You thought I would let your petty thieving slip past without a word, because we're friends; that's presuming a bit far on our friendship though, isn't it? After all, the business belongs to my father; you'd forgotten that, I think. And he's my boss as well as yours—so you see, Marcus, I have no other course but to accuse you."

"But we're brothers! How can you say such a thing as that?" Like a maddened bull, Marcus's booming voice rasped through the still afternoon. "You're one of the family, David—blood-brothers, remember, eh?"

David got up with a quick, sharp movement and stared out of the window. Annie could no longer see his face, but heard the torment in his words. "Yes, I *used* to be one of the family—and I still am, I think, with Mama and the children. But not with you, Marcus. Nor with Katnina. Something's happened, I can feel it, since I was last here. Something's going on . . ."

Turning, he stared across the room, his eyes green and vivid. "Don't bother to deny it. Just explain, if you can."

Marcus's face was a mixture of fury and perplexity. Annie could almost feel his confusion; clearly he didn't know whether to continue with his excuses or answer David's direct question. After a long pause he sat down again, the warm smile appearing very briefly around his mouth as he said quietly, "Perhaps it would be better if you asked Katnina, not me."

Annie caught her breath and looked at David. He was frowning, and she saw a growing belligerence sweep across his lean face. *"Katnina?* What's she got to do with it?"

Marcus waved his hands about placatingly. "Don't look like that! No need to be so angry—not with Katnina. Not after last summer, eh?"

"Go on," said David, waiting.

"But surely there is no need for me to go on, my friend! The family waits for you and she to announce the betrothal day, that's all!" Marcus looked as if he had produced a prize rabbit out of a shabby top hat, and beamed triumphantly.

Annie could stand it no longer. The business confrontation was rapidly sinking into a purely personal quarrel, which was nothing at all to do with her, and everything to do with Katnina. Her heart racing, she got up and collected David's untouched teacup.

"I'll just go and clear this up . . ."

Her feeble excuse was wasted, for neither man seemed to hear or notice her departure. In the kitchen she heard the voices start ranting again, rising and falling, angry words becoming increasingly hate-filled and violent.

She put away the tea things and then loitered in the hallway, willing herself to flee to some safe, quiet place where she could no longer hear them quarrelling. But then David said, loudly and with passion,

"I might have known that Katnina was at the bottom of all this . . ." and her limbs seemed to freeze. She couldn't have moved to save her life.

6

THE verbal violence between the two men seemed to reach out and envelop her—she felt weak and quite unable to even think. So that when finally the voices stopped berating each other and David flung out of the office knocking into her as she stood there, she was in no state to withstand the force of his hurrying body.

Legs and arms entangled as he collided with her. She gasped and would have fallen but for his quick reaction.

"Annie. . . !" Snatched up in his arms, she was lifted off her feet, marched down the hallway and out into the garden, at last being deposited, none too gently, in the passenger seat of the car.

Before she could gather her wits, he had banged the car door, revved the engine and was driving off down the cement track, his jaw uncompromisingly stiff, and the glare in his steely eyes keeping her from asking useless questions.

He drove on, along the curving coast road, in a flurry of dust, ignoring oncoming vehicles and forcing pedestrians to step aside onto the verge. Annie sat there, shocked and anxious, quite incapable of knowing how to cope with this wild side of him. Words simmered in her mind, but she had the sense to keep quiet, knowing with intuitive certainty that silence was what he needed to gain control of himself once again.

At the entrance to the village he slowed down, and she allowed herself the luxury of a long, slow sigh of relief. Perhaps he heard the expellation of breath—he slid a quick sideways glance at her, then returned his eyes to the road. But she saw his lips lift slightly from the down-turned rigidity that the row with Marcus had forced them into. Only then did she dare to speak.

"I'm glad I don't have to drive with you every day."

Somehow she made her voice light and humorous; somehow the right words emerged. She turned her head to smile at his sombre face and realised, thankfully, that she'd done the right thing.

Even as she continued to look at him, he relaxed. The speed of the car lessened, his grip on the wheel became less tight. He allowed himself to smile, a sardonic, self-mocking expression that held a hint of shame. "Well done, Annie. Well done. I knew I could always depend on you." Then he sighed deeply and turned to park the car in a small street where shade fell from high walls enclosing it.

For a moment they sat there in silence, Annie letting the peaceful beauty wash over her, wondering what might happen next after those unexpected words.

What did they mean, she asked herself? *I knew I could always depend on you.* But no answer came to her, and so she merely shook her head, telling herself that all that mattered was that his rage had flown, and that he was glad to have her beside him. She ventured another glance at him, and he smiled more normally in return, a smile that touched her depths and started a glow of happiness bubbling through her body.

He put a hand on hers, as they lay clasped in her lap. "My tower of strength. Thanks, Annie . . . come along, I'll buy you a drink. I think we both need cooling off after that little episode."

The village was coming to life after the siesta hour as David led her along cobbled alleys and streets lined with white-washed walls, while she tried in vain to keep pace with his long steps. She dodged a mule that waited patiently outside a grocery shop, and nearly tripped over innumerable long, thin cats, slinking in and out of the shadows. For a moment she had the ridiculous sense of thinking life was repeating itself, for not many days ago she had been doing this very same thing, trailing behind David Nicholas as he marched angrily through the airport lounge. But so much had happened since that day—she had learned so many lessons, both about him and herself—that now she was able to merely smile at her thoughts, and wait for his unrestrained progress to come to an end.

He stopped in midstep so that she bumped into him as he turned and stared at her, eyes full of apology and humour. Once again their bodies touched, hands trailing and their smiles uniting. He looked shame-faced. "Sorry, Annie, I forgot you were there . . ."

"It's all right. I knew you'd remember —eventually."

They looked deep into each other's eyes. Then he nodded slowly, as if recognising in himself a facet of character that hadn't been obvious before. "God, what a monster I am! Dragging you along here, in all this heat."

"No, you weren't dragging me at all, I came of my own free will." Her words were calm, her face full of contentment. He raised an eyebrow in the usual ironic manner.

"Well, okay if that's how you feel about it, but I'm ashamed of myself, all the same. Let's sit over there by the harbour —you can see the boats while we have a drink."

They sat beneath the shade of a bright umbrella at a small table overlooking the humming waterside. Annie stared with keen interest, for this was the first time she had seen anything of the village, apart from the brief view of it the day they arrived. The *limonada* was refreshing, and she allowed herself to relax, focussing all her concentration on the milling crowds of holiday makers as they wandered past, the varied accents creating a symphony that rose and fell about her ears.

Slowly, she realised the afternoon's emotional scenes had taken a toll of her; now that it was peaceful again, a disquieting sense of weakness overtook her, so that her fingers trembled as she lifted the glass to her mouth. Immediately, David's eyes were full of concern, and his hand reached out to touch hers.

"Are you all right?" Then, as she nodded, "Sure? Promise you'll tell me if you don't feel well? I know what this heat can do when you're not used to it."

The clear anxiety in his eyes baffled her, even as it warmed her heart. Was this really the same man who had locked her bedroom door and looked at her as if she wasn't there? The same David who had, only an hour ago, shouted at Marcus with deep passion in his voice? The man who had gently invited Marcus's daughter to come swimming with him the next morning? Memories zigzagged in front of her eyelids, defeating her determination not to remember; the same David who had kissed her, as she lay on that ridiculous couch in his artist's cabin . . . ?

Confusion forced her to sit back wearily, closing her eyes for a moment. Would she ever understand the opposing parts of this strange, yet undeniably attractive man? She blinked suddenly, as the true knowledge of her deep feelings for him rocketed to the surface; opening her eyes again, she looked straight into his. There was no time for subterfuge, no thought for words that would conceal how she felt.

"David," she murmured faintly, "I want to go home, to go back to England. I must get away from all this . . . I can't cope with it anymore. Please let me go . . ."

His expression mesmerised her, as it changed from concern to disbelief, and then on to impetuous annoyance. The touch of his hand on her passive fingers tightened as he grasped them painfully.

"What on earth are you saying? Don't be silly, Annie! Of course you can't go home—back to cold, wet England and leave this glorious place, where the sun always shines and the sea's warm and . . ."

His lack of understanding came as a blow; the quick temper flared yet again and she cut across his words with a vehemence that made him blink. ". . . and the terrible situation I'm in, slap bang in the middle of a personal vendetta between you and Marcus! Oh, don't deny it, David; I'm not that much of a fool that I can't read between the lines! Of course I know that Marcus has been cheating with the accounts, but you're using that fact to whip up feeling about your own relationship with him . . ." It was on the tip of her tongue to add Katnina's name as well, but mercifully she controlled herself, adding wretchedly, ". . . and I don't want any part in it—so I intend to leave. Even if you say I can't, I shall still go. It's a free world, you don't own me, I only have to pack my bag and book a place on the ferry and . . ."

Amazingly, the contortion of dismay and answering rage left his face. He smiled over the table, mocking her puny anger, still in possession of her hands, yet again the old, arrogant David.

"And sail away, never to be seen again? Come off it, Annie! It's that damned tiger again, isn't it, trying to make himself heard; I never know where I am with you —one minute you're as meek as a mouse and then the next—whew! Explosions!"

"You're a nice one to talk . . . but that's exactly what you do yourself!" She was bewildered, cross at his quick put-down, but, against her will, inevitably succumbing to the high-handed charm that could seemingly be turned on whenever he needed it. She tried to snatch her fingers away from him, but his grip was too strong.

"We seem to have a lot in common . . . go on then, tell me more about myself. It's interesting. I didn't realise you were such a perceptive little thing."

"Don't you dare patronise me, David Nicholas!" Now she was blazingly angry, cheeks highlighted by frustration at not being able to free her hands from his possession. "All right then, if you really want me to, I'll tell you a few home truths. You're spoilt and arrogant, quite incapable of understanding how other people think and feel—you don't seem to mind how you behave. Why, I don't think it even dawns on you that you're so inconsiderate and selfish and—and—"

"Yes?"

"And I'll be extremely glad to finish my work here and go home. If it wasn't for Marcus and his family, I would be having a thoroughly rotten time. You're a very hard task-master, and you don't care a rap about me . . ."

"Of course I don't! Why on earth should I? You're hardly my sort of woman; shrewish, possessed of a vile temper and with no control over it all. What's more, my dear Miss Frayne, you're small-minded to a degree and although I'll grant you have a modicum of attraction in your urchin grin and flaming hair, you're hardly old enough, or experienced enough, to offer anything to a man . . ."

"Oh!" She was furious and hurt at the same time. Both emotions struggled for the whiphand of possession, and to her dismay she felt tears of sheer frustration threatening. David smiled wolfishly.

"So now you know how painful it can be to have your weak spots exposed, don't you, Annie, my love. . . ?"

They glared at each other.

"But you said you wanted to know . . ." she muttered, abruptly impressed by the truth of his argument.

"So I did. I'd almost forgotten."

She looked at him uncertainly. A flicker of mirth gleamed out from the sea-green eyes. Was he laughing at her now?

"I—I—" she stopped and dropped her eyes. From out of the chaos of her emotions answering humour began to emerge, slowly but surely pouring oil on the troubled waters. In a moment they were both laughing; and then she stopped, as an instinctive warning stabbed her relaxing mind.

His hands had crept up her arms, teasing and provoking as they gently stroked the flesh between elbow and wrist. The eyes that could be so hard and frightening were gentle and soft. He said, so quietly, that she could only just hear over the buzz of the busy waterfront crowds, "Any other rude names you want to call me? Don't spare me, Annie . . ."

Ridiculously, tears threatened her. She sniffed, blinked purposefully and muttered in a small, feeble voice, ". . . I was going to say—that—I wish I'd never met you . . ."

She forced herself to return his stare, straining to release her arms from his grasp, forcing her tired mind to resist the charm that crept insidiously in his gently whispered answer.

"Are you quite sure about that, little mouse? Absolutely sure? Because I have my doubts . . ."

Troubled, wondering how he knew the inner recesses of her barricaded emotions, she desperately rallied the last dregs of her waning strength. Her sense of survival brought the flicker of anger into new life. Sharply, she said, "And now you're being patronising again! Just because every other girl you meet falls for that heady charm of yours, you think I've done so as well."

Abruptly he sat back, freeing her arms, distancing himself with a face that had become suddenly cold. "I see."

She caught her breath in distress. How could she hurt him so? Only a few minutes ago she had faced the awful fact that she loved him . . . but even so, he mustn't be allowed to make use of her; she was a person, not a mere convenience. Confusion swept through her as she watched the expression in his veiled eyes. Without knowing what she was saying, she started to give in.

"I'm sorry, David, I've said some awful things, I know, but you did push me . . ."

Silence, broken only by the melée of foreign accents that filled the air. She watched a small boy unloading fish from a swaying, blue-painted caique moored at the quayside, hardly noticing the huge eye that decorated its prow; tensely she waited for David's *coup-de-grace.*

But when at last he spoke, it was far from the put-down she had expected. "Yes, Annie, I know I did. And I'm sorry."

She stared in surprise as he got to his feet and came around to stand behind her chair, hands lightly touching her shoulders, his voice very intimate, his mouth close to her ear. "I've given you a hard time; I'm a brute and I know it . . . forgive me?"

Head whirling, she turned to face him. What could she say? Only one thing, feeling about him as she did. Her tired voice murmured wearily, "There's nothing to forgive, David . . ."

His smile caught her up, giving her new vitality, new hope; hand beneath her elbow, he guided her along the quayside, pointing out the little shops that stood, like dark, inviting caves, spilling their wares into the brilliant sunshine.

"You said you needed to buy some postcards, well, here's your chance. Let's see what they've got . . ."

The shops were filled with treasures cunningly displayed to separate the world's currency from visiting holidaymakers. Annie sighed with enjoyment at all she saw, the infinite variety of goods, colours, fragrances and crafts slowly recharging her spirits, and helping to dispel the memories of the long, traumatic afternoon.

"This would suit you . . ." David pointed at a hand-woven peasant tunic in a subtly rich shade of dark green. "Just your colour; take an artist's advice." He smiled at her as if the rough words they had recently thrown at each other had never been said.

"Yes, it's lovely; but this is even nicer . . ." A finely pleated cotton dress, ravishing in its natural elegance, swayed gracefully on its hanger and Annie's eyes lit up, recognising, as every woman does, the one garment that has been fashioned solely for her. "What do you think?" She held up the dress, wondering, even as she spoke, at the amazing fact that here she was, shopping with David, asking for his comments, quite ready to accept without demur whatever he said; it was incredible. What on earth was happening to her? She smiled up at him, knowing the truth was visible in her eyes, and yet unable to mask it.

"I think you'll look absolutely marvellous in it. Quite irresistible, in fact. Put it on, wear it straight away, and then we'll have supper somewhere where you can be admired . . . go on, Annie."

Beguiled by his quiet persuasion, by the intimacy of his words and the certainty behind them, she did as he suggested, emerging from behind the skimpily concealing curtain at the back of the shop a few minutes later knowing he had been right. Even in the half-light, with the aid of a cracked, side-tilted mirror, she had seen, without unnecessary false modesty, that the dress did a lot for her. It was hers; it made her glow, brought her to life.

David waited outside, intent at a stand of paperbacks. She paid for the dress, exchanging friendly sign language with the shop owner. Suddenly embarrassed and unsure, she joined him in the sunshine, waiting as he flicked over the pages of the book in his hand. He turned, and with a leaping heart she watched his eyes widen, then narrow again, the bright sea colour made even more vivid by a certain light that shone, deep within them. "Lovely," he said slowly, his gaze going down from her tense face to the sunburned legs and then returning to the bare, golden arms and shoulders. "You look a picture, my dear Miss Frayne . . ."

There was a little moment of silence. Then, "Th—thank you," whispered Annie.

He took her hand. "Come along, Cinderella, we're off to the ball—not that my finery can compare with yours, but then, who'll bother to look at me when you're so utterly ravishing?"

"Now you're being ridiculous."

Warm fingers pressed hers warningly.

"No more psychology, please. Enough's enough. Let's forget we're such sworn enemies—tonight we'll be friends for a change."

She made no response, but the feeling of well-being that was filling her increased. David tugged at her hand until she was forced to look at him. "Or, of course, if you're in the mood—and you only have to say so—we could even be lovers; just for tonight."

His mockery would have wounded her earlier today; now, full of the knowledge she was learning about him, she understood that such mockery was a facade behind which his own strangely vulnerable emotions frequently hid. So she took the remark calmly and told herself to stay alert and passive, for this was only one more of his sophisticated jokes. He was merely entertaining her as he knew best, certainly not meaning anything deeper than that.

"Let's leave it at friendship, shall we? I'll call a truce for that," she replied lightly, and was able to smile quite casually, commending herself for the new measure of self control suddenly within reach.

The sky was already touched with the first gentle signs of sunset, a pale apricot light creating a mystery in the golden west. They walked on, silent but, Annie felt, sharing a bond of enjoyment in the beauty of the dying day. Shops gave way to fish-cellars and boat-houses, and at last David stopped outside a large, white stone building that looked like a converted warehouse.

"Here we are—in you go, Annie."

On the threshold she paused for a second, staring back over her shoulder, reluctant to leave the vivid beauty staining the heavens. A brilliance of orange shot with gold lit up the far horizon, fading through the gamut of fiery colours until, towards the east, the sky grew shadowy and lowering, tones and half-tones of grey giving way to indigo and, finally, to the impenetrable black of oncoming night.

She tore her eyes away from the breath-taking spectacle, to find him watching her closely. "It's so beautiful," she murmured and he nodded.

"Even better when you're in the middle of it. I'll take you out in the boat one evening and you can see for yourself—would you like that?"

Once again indecision stalked her. She longed to accept the invitation but knew that if she had any sense—and she was fast wondering if there was any left, within her—she would resolutely stay away from such experiences. The sea at sunset, with David? Not if she could help it. So she left the question unanswered, stepping past him into the big building and glad of the diversion of the greeting that rang out at once.

"Good evening, Madame—ah, David, my friend!"

A handsome young Greek bowed to her and then, in a burst of recognition, pulled David into a close hug.

"Hallo, Niko. Good to see you again. Can we have a table in the corner? Somewhere quiet, but with a good view of the cabaret . . ."

"For you, David, I have just the table. I change a reservation—see—no one will know!" Grinning, Niko removed a card from the table he led them to and put it on another close by, half-hidden behind a pillar supporting a vigorous growth of some fleshy indoor plant.

Seated, Annie looked about her with interest, as David ordered drinks and discussed the menu. From the appearance of the people already seated in alcoves and shaded corners of the long, elegantly decorated room, she guessed that this restaurant was the haunt of the motley of moneyed, international visitors to the island. There was an atmosphere about the place, a sense of affluence and sophistication that was strangely alien to the native primitiveness of Doloffinos.

The women seated around the room appeared to her as exotic birds of paradise, so colourful and richly varied were the dresses, pants-suits, shawls and shining jewels that they displayed, all set to perfection by gleaming suntans. Beside such paragons of *haute couture* their escorts were merely dun-coloured and ordinary.

For a moment Annie flinched, glancing down at her own cheap, island-cotton turquoise dress; she couldn't hope to compare with such startling glamour, but then, unbidden, came the memory of the look in David's eyes as she had come out of the shop in her new finery. As she remembered, her head rose proudly. He had said that she was lovely, and so she had no reason to worry.

He caught her eye. "I ordered some retsina for us both—you don't mind? It's the local wine and quite palatable once you get used to the rather unusual taste. You can't possibly visit Greece and not try it. Are you hungry?"

Feeling unexpectedly relaxed, she smiled back happily. "Starving, actually. What did Niko recommend?"

"The lobster."

"Sounds good." Her gaze briefly circled the room again, then returned to him. "This is quite a place—I've never seen so many diamonds on so many elegant women in my life before! I suppose this is the in-place eating house?"

He accepted the wine from Niko and nodded at Annie as her glass was filled. "That's about it. From all over the world they come in their thousands to see who can win the prize for over-dressing *Chez Niko!* Drink up and see if you like this. Slowly now, it's got quite a bite . . ."

He watched her concernedly as she first

smelled, then sipped the wine, and she realised with a sudden impact that at this particular moment he had no eyes nor thoughts for anyone in the room but herself. It was a heady idea, and beneath his friendly gaze she felt herself blossoming; no longer half-mouse, half-tiger, but just Annie herself, at ease with a man whose company she was enjoying.

The music added to her pleasure as the evening wore on. The violins and bouzouki played ceaselessly, providing a background to the hum of voices that chattered over their meals; but occasionally it cast a spell on its listeners, calling them out onto the tiny floor to dance their hearts out in spontaneous expressions of joy.

Annie watched the linked arms, the stamping feet and happiness of the swaying, music-charmed dancers with envy, not aware of David's eyes on her face. When he touched her arm and said, "Like to have a go?" she was delighted, but suddenly reluctant to make an exhibition of herself.

"I don't know if I can—"

"Nonsense. You'll find the steps dance

themselves. Just give yourself to the music."

She found herself in a line of smiling strangers who made willing space for her, and drew into the dance. With David on one side and a young, dark-haired Turkish boy on the other, suddenly her feet fell into the pattern of steps without any trouble: she swung and swayed, caught in a rhythm that had first caught fire at the beginning of time. Delight filled her and when, as the music ended, David led her back to their table, she felt she was still treading a measure, relaxed and sure of herself, happy as never before.

After the lobster came fresh fruit, and then David signalled Niko to bring huge glasses of brandy, smiling into her eyes as she shook her head. "Don't worry, I won't let you get drunk. You can trust me to look after you. Ah, here's the cabaret . . ."

The lights went down and a buzz of interest circled the room as a flamboyant trill from the bouzouki heralded the arrival of a girl dressed spectacularly in a full-pleated skirt of shot silk, topped with a gold-stitched bolero. The raven-black hair was swept back and built up and decorated with scarlet ribbons. Annie sipped the brandy dubiously, then decided its fiery trickle was pleasant, and settled down to be entertained.

The girl danced like an angel, her movements one long cord of sinuous self-control. Annie's eyes quickened—surely she recognised that heart-shaped face, the subtle smile that flickered in and out, like the sun's rays on a cloudy day? A finger of chill discontent ran through her body as realisation came. *Katnina.*

Now she realised why David had chosen to bring her here. Not, as she had foolishly and self-indulgently chosen to think, to please her, but rather to see Katnina, whom he loved.

From that moment on, until the dance ended, Annie's pleasure left her. And when, flushed and smiling, more beautiful than ever in her triumph, Katnina bowed low to the audience and then wove her way through the applauding tables towards them, actual pain began to rack her.

But it was nothing to the stab of cold, cruel jealousy that she experienced when Katnina came to their table, her lovely face

163

illumined by a smile that outshone the artifice and mere surface glamour of her jewelled costume.

"Ah, David, thank you for coming," she murmured, and without hesitation lifted her face for his kiss, as he put his arms about her.

7

THE evening was over, David sitting on the starlit terrace at the villa with a last cigar and a nightcap, and Annie again alone in her bedroom.

Somehow she had endured his casual introduction to Katnina, who had smiled politely, and then proceeded to engage him in a conversation which entirely precluded Annie. Somehow she had kept a fixed expression of agreeable pleasure on her frozen face as he drove her home, after leaving Katnina chatting to Niko before going backstage and resting, ready for her second appearance in the small hours.

They had said goodnight at the villa entrance, David looking at Annie with sober eyes and a gentle expression that had forced her to clip short her thanks and bang the door of the bedroom behind her.

She showered and got ready for bed thinking numbly that she must endure the rest of her visit to Doloffinos without revealing to anybody—and particularly

David—that she was miserably unhappy and would never feel quite the same again.

For she had done exactly what he had warned her against. Staring out of the window into the velvety night, Annie allowed herself a feeble smile of self-ridicule. He had said *don't allow your emotions to become involved*—but whereas he had warned her against Marcus and the family up in the mountains, he hadn't thought to mention his own name.

What a fool she was, oh, *what* a fool; naive, inexperienced, jumping with both feet into water that was bottomless and disturbed. She had only herself to blame. He had warned her and she had chosen to disregard his words, showing an arrogance that matched his own. Well, it was over now. She had learned so much about herself that had never even been guessed at before she came to Doloffinos—that she was an emotional, sensual creature, who reacted all too easily to the assaults of beauty, wonder and physical stimuli . . . for a long, wounding moment she recalled David's nearness, his hands on hers, his mouth tasting her own, and then, with a supreme burst of self-preservation, she gave a little half-sob as she closed the shutters on the treacherously evocative night, and went to bed.

In the morning she wondered how her reflection in the mirror could appear so normal; clear eyes and a curving lift to her mouth that betrayed nothing of the stupendous sorrow and emptiness within her.

It was a relief of a sort—to know that she could carry off the situation without giving way, finishing the work she was here to do, remaining on friendly terms with everybody and even perhaps giving Alexa a small boost of encouragement before the ferry and the plane took her out of harm's way, back to London and out of David's life for ever. For of course he would forget her once she was back in the Accounts Department—why should he remember?

She toyed with her breakfast and was glad that Marcus had arrived early, clearly making an effort towards reconciliation by trying to keep David occupied with rambling reminiscences of their shared boyhood.

"—and what about the time we went to

Voolani, where the goats pasture in the summer, and stayed for two nights, fishing for our food and cooking on an open fire? And Katnina came over with Yannos in the evenings with the wine—it was a happy time. I shall never forget such days, David—nor you, eh?"

Annie, assembling her ledgers and invoices, wished she could work elsewhere, but was forced to sit there and listen to David's seemingly reluctant reply.

"That was a very long time ago. We were only children then." She wondered idly why he was so unwilling to share Marcus's nostalgia.

"Not so—I was a man, you were a man; ask Katnina if you weren't!" Marcus guffawed and she glanced at David, whose face was abruptly tensed with quick anger.

"I've told you, we were all little better than children then—Katnina and I were friends, but nothing more. What the hell do you mean?"

"Don't lose your temper! You and Katnina were fond of each other then—as you still are, my friend. That's so, isn't it?"

Marcus's deep voice was full of laughter,

but Annie detected a subtle note of intrigue as well; it dawned on her that he was being altogether too insistent about the relationship between David and his sister. Thinking back, she recalled how he had teased Katnina about her forthcoming betrothal, then remembered David's warm embrace of Katnina last night. She waited unhappily for his answer, forcing her eyes to stare at the column of figures in the book, while her heart beat too fast and all her thoughts held their breaths.

"Fond of each other?" David's sharp words became a question, hanging in the hot, sunny room. "Of course we're *fond of each other . . .*" The emphasis was hard and aggressive. "What are you getting at, Marcus?"

"Why, only that, naturally, you want her to be happy—in order to be happy yourself."

"And what's that supposed to mean, for God's sake? Stop beating about the bush, can't you?"

Annie scraped back her chair. It was no good, she just couldn't sit there and hear David assure Marcus that he loved Katnina and meant to marry her. Very fast, and on the spur of the moment, she said, "I've just remembered that Alexa is outside, and so I think I'll go and see her. She may be wondering if we've forgotten about her swim . . ."

"Good idea." David seemed as relieved as she was that the conversation had come to such unexpected end. "Tell her we'll be out in a minute. Now Marcus, back to business—did you deal with that broken shutter yesterday? I don't want the owner to have to complain again . . ."

Thankfully Annie escaped, to find Alexa sitting on the grass in the shade of a huge oleander bush not far from the villa. The child's pensive face lit up as Annie appeared and called to her.

"Alexa! Hallo! All ready for your swim? David's coming soon. Tell me how your leg feels this morning?"

"Rather funny. As if it forgets how to walk."

Alexa stroked her leg anxiously and Annie said stoutly, "Well, it's time it remembered! And some exercise in the sea is just what it needs. Have you got your swimming suit?"

"Under my dress. It's a new one." Proudly the child lifted her skirt.

"My word, that's a smart one. Was it a present?"

"Papa bought it—he said it will help me get better to have a new suit to swim in. He always gives me presents, my Papa."

Yes, thought Annie dryly—using the Villa Estate funds to do so. She wondered if David had any idea of the poverty in which the islanders lived before the tourist industry brought the extra drachma which made such a difference to their simple lives? But of course he must do—hadn't he lived here himself, sharing his childhood with Marcus and his family? So why couldn't he work out for himself the reason for the embezzling?

Suddenly his shadow fell across the parched grass and his voice said commandingly, "Come on, you two, the sea's waiting. Annie, carry the flippers and the mask, will you? Alexa, I'll give you a piggy-back, up with you."

There was much laughter and good-natured chaff between the two of them as David carried his excited burden down to the beach, finally depositing her on the sand only a few yards from the sea. Alexa tore off her dress, put on the flippers and mask and, leaving her crutches behind, hopped into the water with Annie close behind her and David's arm firmly about the child's waist.

"A bit further out—here, let me tow you. Just relax, Alexa—give me your hand. That's it. Here we go."

Alexa trusted him completely, thought Annie, following behind with a sedate breast-stroke. It was good of him to desert the office and the thousand-and-one affairs that must be waiting to be decided upon; to give his precious time to one small girl with a weak leg whose frail body, for some reason, refused to heal. Annie's brows creased as she swam. Was it at all possible that Alexa's problem lay in the fact that she knew Marcus was involved in theft? Had she, at some time or other, overheard unthinking talks which revealed the unsavoury truth? Could it be this worry which lay like a cloud over her childish mind, keeping her recovery at bay? Annie knew that many ailments are caused by unquiet minds—now she wondered, with fresh insight, if this was indeed the case with Alexa.

But already the snorkelling lesson had begun. "Annie—support her legs and gently help them to flip up and down. It's okay, Alexa, I've got you round the middle, you can't possibly sink. Put your head down and move your feet—well, what can you see down there?"

Alexa gurgled rather breathlessly and began to thrash about with her one strong leg, while the other one remained helplessly stiff. Annie did as she was told, and carefully encouraged the poor, wasted limb to move in time with the good one. Soon Alexa was improving.

"Excellent. Try a bit harder—that's it. Well done, we'll have you practising for the Olympics before you know it!" David sounded like a fond elder brother, and Annie warmed to him once again. After some twenty minutes' exercise he took Alexa back to the shore, and Annie turned on her back, floating on the lilting waves alone.

Their voices faded, replaced by the singing waters lapping her relaxed body. Her anxieties left her as she shut her eyes serenely beneath the sun's fierce glare. What a strange world it was out here, clasped in Poseidon's arms . . . time ended as she lay there, and when David suddenly surfaced a few feet away, she was catapulted back into reality with a jolt.

"What are you thinking about, mermaid?" He trod water beside her, flicking wet hair out of his eyes, and she was too overcome to answer anything but the truth.

"That I could easily stay here for ever. It's so wonderful."

"And yet only yesterday you were pleading to be allowed to go home—why the sudden change of heart?"

"Well . . ." Lying there on her back, with his head so close to hers that his breath brushed her cheek, she searched his eyes doubtfully, but, finding only friendliness there, was encouraged to go on honestly.

"Well, yesterday afternoon was terrible. You and Marcus fighting . . . And I just couldn't bear to think of him being caught stealing, and what that would do to his family."

"And today it doesn't matter any

longer? Poor old Marcus, he'd be so hurt if he knew you didn't care about him any longer."

She caught the quiet mockery and said indignantly, letting her legs go down so that she could face him more directly, "Of course it still matters. But at least today I understand *why* he had to steal."

"Really? Such powers of intuition. Tell me, Annie."

Noticing with a sudden stab of appreciation that his eyes were the same colour as the water that bore him up, she said calmly "Because of Alexa, of course. He's had so many things to pay for since the accident—her operation—oh, all sorts of expenses that he could never manage on his salary alone."

For a long moment David returned her stare, and then, as if by mutual consent, they both turned and began leisurely swimming back towards the shore, where Alexa sat and waved.

Thoughtfully, between strokes, David said, "But he earns a very good salary," and Annie stopped in mid-stroke to face him again.

"Yes, but surely you realise he supports

his whole family? And I don't suppose it's enough to pay for all the extras that have been needed lately."

Their bodies merged beneath the water's wavering shadows, and Annie caught her breath as he brushed her shoulder, saying, with a strange expression in his vivid eyes, "Got it all worked out, haven't you? Marcus is the poor peasant and I'm the rich, uncaring capitalist employer . . . you've certainly got a genius for putting me in the wrong, Annie."

She shied away from the stare that had suddenly become an accusing one, and with a burst of energy catapulted herself away from him, calling over her shoulder, "If you're trying to start another argument, well, I'm not playing. Everything was so lovely just now, I don't want it to change . . ."

When she walked, dripping and a little breathless, both from her exertions and her suddenly churning emotions, up the beach to where Alexa sat, she was unaware that David hadn't followed her in. As she turned to look for him, she saw his sleek head slowly becoming more and more difficult to see as the moments passed.

A feeling of uneasiness swept through her, but then she picked up her towel, purposefully putting him from her mind. If he wanted to sulk, well let him—she just didn't care any more.

Beside her, Alexa said perceptively, "Why are you unhappy, Annie? Because David is not here?"

Quickly she looked down at the child's upraised face, and forced a smile. "Of course not! And I'm not unhappy—whatever made you think I was?"

Alexa let a palmful of silvery sand drop from one small hand to the other before she replied, hesitantly, "Because you have a feeling about you—a not-happy feeling. I can tell, like I do with Papa sometimes, when he comes from the villa after he works on his accounts. I don't like people to be unhappy." She raised suddenly pleading eyes and Annie, deeply touched, knelt down at her side, smiling reassuringly back.

"Neither do I, Alexa, love—that makes two of us. And two people are stronger than one, any day—so let's both put our minds to making everybody happy, shall we?"

"Of course. But how?"

"By you getting better, and me going back to the office and getting on with my work. I think we've been here long enough now. Ups-a-daisy!"

Alexa struggled to her feet, reaching for the crutches that leaned against the nearby rock. "Will I get better, Annie? Sometimes I think never."

Annie, with her arm supporting the child's waist, gave her a playful shake, even as her heart raced with dismay. "You think too much, you little silly! Why not use all that energy in a far better way, exercising your leg—why, we'll have you throwing those old crutches away long before I leave the island . . ."

"Leave? But you can't leave! You've only just come—" Alexa stopped her halting progress up the beach to stare tragically at Annie.

"It's all right, I'm not going for at least another week." Annie felt a stab of concern. Why should Alexa be so loth to see her go? The child had a loving family, she was cared for and cossetted, everyone seemingly doing all they could to speed her recovery. So why such a heartfelt plea? It wasn't natural for the child to cling to a mere acquaintance like herself, surely . . .

But she knew it wasn't the time to think of such things. Alexa must be returned to Marcus, and then she must get on with her work. She was relieved to see the child's sombre mood abruptly change to one of gaiety as Marcus tenderly put her into the car, prior to going home to lunch. Alexa prattled on about the excitement of the swim, and what she had seen through the snorkel mask.

"And tomorrow you will do it again. Why, in no time your leg will be strong and you'll be running around instead of using these things, my little love." Marcus threw the crutches onto the back seat, smiled at Annie and started the engine.

"Goodbye, Annie—I will see you tomorrow, yes?"

"Of course, Alexa. Cheerio for now."

Annie watched the little head looking back over its shoulder, and the hand waving madly until the car disappeared up the hill, then went indoors to speedily shower and change, before immersing herself yet again in the world of unreconciled figures.

Later she was startled to hear approaching steps in the hallway and a piercing, transatlantic voice behind her, saying loudly, "Do forgive me, my dear, I walked right in. I was hoping to see David—isn't he about?"

Annie looked around. In the doorway stood a middle-aged woman of immense elegance and presence. Her carefully-dressed hair was the same soft grey-blue as her stylishly cut sundress, and a diamond that surely rivalled the one belonging to Elizabeth Taylor glinted on her left hand.

"He's out at the moment," said Annie, intrigued. "Perhaps I can help you?" Getting to her feet, she offered the newcomer a chair.

"How thoughtful! Of course, I should really be on the yacht with my friends, but with the party so near there's a lot to do, and it was only by the sheerest chance that I learned dear David was here at all. Strange that he hasn't been to see me, he always did in other years . . . Not expected at this time of the season, was he? Marcus didn't mention that he was coming. Oh, but I should have introduced myself, I'm Sharon Potter. Hiram—that's my husband—and I rent the Villa Mirama —but you're new here aren't you, my dear? I haven't seen you before."

Politely Annie waited for the spate of words to end. She smiled at the curious face looking up at her and said, "I'm Annie Frayne. I came with Mr. Nicholas a few days ago to help in the office."

"His secretary! And you're English! That lovely, cool accent—so attractive, I always think. And you've got such beautiful hair . . . David must be delighted to have you with him, my dear."

Annie found the knowing smile and the innuendo distasteful. "I only work for him," she said coldly.

"Of course," cooed Mrs. Potter. "But all work makes Annie a dull girl, eh?" Her smirk nudged Annie into action, who efficiently reached for pen and paper.

"If you have a message, I'll let David see it directly he returns, Mrs. Potter. I'm sure you don't want to waste any more time, as you're so busy."

"You're so right, my dear. Just tell the darling boy that I expect to see him at my beach party. Why—why, David, there you are!"

His bare feet had made no sound as he entered, appearing suddenly in the doorway behind them. Annie opened her mouth to give the required message, but Mrs. Potter forestalled her, rising at once and going to stand beside him, her smile a little too friendly, her voice a fraction too coy.

"You naughty boy, you haven't been to see me this year." She touched his arm with pudgy fingers.

"I apologise, Sharon. I only got here a couple of days ago and there's been a lot to do." Annie sensed his innate politeness masking a very real dislike.

"Like swimming?" Mrs. Potter's china blue eyes swept over his drying trunks and the traces of silver sand still clinging to his bare legs.

A muscle in his cheek twitched ominously. "That and other things."

A shiver ran through Annie. She knew that he was rapidly losing patience with the importunate, foolish woman, and was glad not to be on the receiving end of his displeasure. She tried to cover the awkward moment of silence. "Mrs. Potter called in to invite you to her beach party, David."

Sliding his veiled, careful eyes across to her, he said, "But how kind."

"Now, you just have to come, David, you always do, and I shan't take no for an answer." Mrs. Potter's voice grew honeysweet. "And of course the invite includes dear Katnina—as usual."

David's arm moved, and her diamond-gleaming hand fell away. He crossed the room swiftly on the pretext of draping his towel over the back of a chair. Casually he turned. "Very good of you Sharon, but I happen to know that Katnina won't be able to come. And I myself have another appointment, I'm afraid."

"Nonsense!" cried Mrs. Potter firmly. "Put it off! This is the beach party of the season! The annual event all the Estate visitors look forward too—why, David, if you don't come, they might just think something was wrong; that perhaps the management had lost interest in them— and you wouldn't want that to happen, I'm sure. As it is, none of us seem to have seen very much of Marcus this summer; one can't help wondering a little. But there, that's none of my business, is it . . . so for goodness' sake make up your mind to come—and bring your little English friend with you."

David's eyes sought out Annie, who stared back, embarrassed and non-plussed. If he expected her to accept the invitation, then he was quite wrong; it was the last thing in the world that she wanted, to have her name coupled with his. She shook her head mutely, and watched his gaze return to Mrs. Potter, who was looking at her jewelled watch.

"My word, I had no idea it was so late. I really must get on—so much to do, you know. Goodbye, David darling. Goodbye, Miss—er—Frayne, wasn't it? Until Saturday evening, then, my dears . . ."

She went off smiling, with David politely escorting her, the piercing voice still audible after she had left the villa. Annie remained where she was, uneasily wondering what David would have to say when he returned. Tension began to fill her anew; yet another unhappy situation was growing up between them—would it never end?

He stamped back into the office. "Damned woman! I have this trouble every year with her blasted party—thought I'd avoided it this time by not being here. One more thing Marcus has got to answer for . . ."

Sitting down, he pulled across to him the ledger on which she had been working so recently. "Haven't you finished this yet?"

The sun shone about him, making a halo of his bright hair. Annie's resolve, like her legs, turned to jelly. He looked up and caught her eye and she felt her cheeks grow hot.

"I—I was getting on quite well until she —Mrs. Potter—came . . ."

His frown fled and he smiled, thawing her nervousness. "Poor Annie! Just one thing after another, isn't it? Tell you what, let's have a drink before lunch. Like to go and pour them while I get the salt and sand off me?"

"Of course." Like a robot, she made her way to the kitchen and was just coming out again with a tray of drinks, when

David emerged from his own room. His hair was still damp, curling in small glistening bunches behind his ears. The trunks were replaced by sleek white linen slacks that emphasised the golden tan of his bare muscular arms beneath a short-sleeved black silk shirt. Once again his natural charisma reached out to draw her, like a magnet, but she was at last learning how to deal with her errant impulses.

Unfalteringly she put the drinks on a small table and then retreated to the chair furthest away from his on the terrace.

"Thanks." His eyes followed her. They looked at each other warily, assessing the situation, and she was the one to turn away first.

"Well." His voice was cool and speculative as he sipped his drink. "Have you got something pretty to wear to the old girl's do? Who knows, you might even enjoy it. After all, we don't have to spend the whole evening in her company—or that of her boring friends—do we?"

Halfway to her own glass Annie stared in amazement. "But surely—I mean, you don't really want me to come, do you?"

"Why not?" No longer could she resist the magnetic force of his eyes.

"Because . . ." Her voice faltered. Unhappily she sensed that he was enjoying her obvious dismay, and the fact made her lapse into silence.

But he wouldn't let her off the hook. "Because what, Annie? Because you don't want to spend the evening with *me*, is that it?"

The truth hit her hard, forcing her to cover up shakily. "It's not that at all."

"Well, what then?"

She searched wildly for excuses, and words came tumbling out in an uncontrollable spate of hurt pride and pain. "I thought you'd probably much rather take Katnina; surely she can have an evening off when she wants?"

The name hung between them in the warm air and Annie drank her *limonada* wretchedly, abruptly wishing it was hemlock. What a fool she was to antagonise him so—couldn't she ever keep her mouth shut? But, instead of dying, she merely spluttered into her drink when he answered, with far more self-control than she would have thought possible, under such blatant attack, "Oh no, Katnina wouldn't be nearly as much fun on a beach party as you, Annie, love; I mean, she's done it all before. This will be a new experience for you. For us."

She looked at him, held against her will by the hint of amusement in his voice. The sea-green eyes mocked a little as he went on, "So just make up your mind that you're coming. And now, if you've quite finished choking over your lemonade, I suggest we go and see what Anthula's put out for lunch, shall we?"

8

OVER lunch David was thoughtful and not inclined to talk, but as Annie got up to take the empty plates back to the kitchen, he caught her eye.

"Annie, you can have the afternoon off. I need time to myself, to think over one or two things—I'll probably go down to the cabin and fiddle around with my paints, clean a few brushes . . . do you drive? You can take my car if you like."

"Oh, no!" She couldn't really see herself driving the fast blue convertible with any degree of confidence—and supposing she damaged it? Smiling a quick apology she added, "I mean, it's kind of you, but I'd rather try my luck with the 'bus; I've seen one going along the road in the early part of the afternoon. Are you sure you don't need me here?"

"No, go and enjoy yourself." Already, she could see, he was withdrawing into his own private world of business negotiations and worries, his face set and lost in thought. Her heart swelled with sympathy —if only he would talk to her, confide his troubles . . . but why should he? No doubt he already had a loving confidante in Katnina.

Her thoughts got the better of her. Impulsively she said, "I do hope you'll—" and then bit her tongue, but it was too late to recall the words. He turned and stared.

"Go on—finish what you were saying."

She looked away from his probing eyes and muttered hesitantly, "I was only hoping that you wouldn't decide to have another row with Marcus. I know it's no business of mine, but—"

"On the contrary it has a lot to do with you. You're the one who's discovered so many of his discrepancies, so you're just as involved as I am. And you have a personal feeling towards him, too—thanks, Annie, I'll think about your advice. In fact, I'll think about several things you've said, just lately . . ."

She dared to raise her eyes, then, not sure if he was mocking her or not, but the expression on his face was perceptive, if sombre. He smiled very briefly and again

190

her sympathy prodded her to add, "Well, I'm glad about that. Not that my advice can have any real bearing on your decision of course—but it's nice of you to listen."

"Not at all. Got any more ideas while you're about it?"

She wondered at the sincerity of his words, but took the opportunity, regardless, to air the fears which crowded her restless mind. "Yes I have, actually."

David rose and went to the edge of the terrace, staring out to sea. "Go ahead, then."

She hesitated, searching for the right words. "I do so hope that your decision won't be the one I fear it might . . ."

He turned and a small, wry smile lifted his straight mouth. "That's a bit Irish, isn't it?"

"What I mean is . . ." She floundered hopelessly for a moment, and then let it all come out in a rush, just as she felt it.

"Please don't sack Marcus." Dismayed, she watched his face again set in the heavy, obstinate lines, the old expression of remembered arrogance making him untouchable and distant.

"And what if I do? How can I go on

191

employing a man who's fast cheating the business of every penny it makes?" he said defensively.

"But you're exaggerating! The whole amount is only just over a thousand pounds!" Once again his coldness was tinder to her sharp temper. She heard herself answering back in no uncertain terms and felt dismayed, but it was said; she had nothing more to lose, so why not go on and get it all out into the open?

"And—and Marcus and his family are my friends, and I don't want them to have to suffer any more, which they will do if you sack him . . ."

He snapped back at her instantly. "Suffer? Don't be so bloody silly! You talk as if we were back in the days of the industrial revolution; just because Marcus may have to find a new job won't cause his family any 'suffering' . . ."

His obvious contempt fanned the flame even more. "You don't know anything about it! If you did you wouldn't be so hurtful and unthinking! You live in top hotels, on yachts and luxurious holiday villas—how can you possibly know about poverty, living as you do?"

"Good God!" He glowered at her, but she refused to be silenced now.

Her emotions had been so churned up since arriving on the island that she knew she could control them no longer. Things were much better brought to the surface than locked away, unspoken; they festered and caused untold future pain if not released. And even if he never spoke to her again, at least she knew she had done the right thing in getting it all off her chest.

He muttered something and she said, after a short pause, "I'm sorry, I didn't catch what you said . . ."

His eyes were like swords and the expression on his face was that of a man not only angry but immensely unhappy. Sharply and with heavy emphasis, he answered, "I merely said that one can easily live in luxury and yet experience untold poverty in other spheres of life . . . but I don't expect you to understand a word of that; you've made up your mind that I'm a scoundrel and that's what you'll continue to think."

She was in such a state of anger and bewilderment that at the time his meaning passed over her head; all she could think of was the imminent fate of Marcus and his family. Words poured out again.

"Marcus told me that you were as good as brought up together, but it's clear that you've forgotten a lot that you learned in those days; about how poor the islanders are, and how much they depend on the Villa Estate for well-paid jobs. If you do kick Marcus out, he'll have to go back to fishing and growing vegetables, and he's got a mother, two brothers, a sister *and* an invalid daughter all depending on him. Just think about that before you make such a heartless decision!"

Dizzily, she wondered at her own impudence. No good could surely come of such foolishness as telling the boss's son what to do—nothing would change David, once his mind was made up, as well she knew. The only ultimate result might be her own dismissal, along with Marcus's. It looked as if she had signed a deathwarrant—for a moment her heart sank and she began to regret the impulsive outburst; but then, logic won the day. It was done and she was glad she had been so frank, come what may. So why worry?

She became aware of David's eyes fastened on her face, caught in a tangle with her own, their silence tautening into an almost physical cloud of antipathy. Fascinated, she watched a muscle move in his bronzed, lean cheek, watched his eyes blaze with something surely very closely akin to hatred . . . her heart beat a rapid tattoo of apprehension. But her courage held, and her own stare didn't waver as she held his.

At last he turned away, abrupt and dismissing. Slowly, Annie allowed herself to unwind a little, wondering anew at the unexpected bravery she had just displayed, even though she had no illusions as to the outcome of such misguided idealism.

"Don't miss that 'bus," David's impersonal voice came from a great distance, returning her to the immediacy of the present.

"No—I won't . . ." Before she reached the entrance to the hall he spoke again, making her stop and turn in amazement.

"Annie—one last thing, before you go. You've just shown how very understanding you are, and what you said is maybe true, that I've forgotten much of what I once knew when Marcus and I were boys together. So I'm grateful to you for reminding me of that. But this gift of yours—understanding people . . . don't you think you should use it much more indiscriminately? I mean, it isn't always the poor and the obviously suffering who need such sympathy, you know—couldn't you spread it around a bit more?"

The quiet, deeply felt words touched her heart. Staring, she saw on his face an expression that she had never noticed before; humility? Concern? Could it be pain?

Words failed her. She was totally unprepared for such an about-face. What was it that he wanted of her? If he couldn't tell her, then she was unable to guess . . . and oh, how tired she was of these interminable emotional outbursts . . .

Unable to meet the challenge in those mesmeric sea-green eyes, she shook her head and left the terrace without looking back, went to her room and hurriedly got together the things needed for an afternoon in the village. Then, leaving the villa like a shadow slipping away, she went down the track onto the dusty, hot road, and waited for the 'bus to come and rescue her.

The sun beat down out of the vivid, unclouded sky, and she felt careworn and bemused. Did she have the energy to go into the village and mix with the chattering crowds, in and out of the shops, climbing the white-washed alleys to visit the church, maybe walking beyond the harbour to the little boatyard around the next scallop of coastline?

As the minutes passed, without any sign of the 'bus, so Annie accepted that she would rather spend her few hours' freedom in the shade, away from the glaring sunlight. She wandered down the road and turned off to the left, along a dusty, narrow track edged with sparse, burned grass, and a few straggling olive trees. It was quiet and she could go at her own pace . . . gradually the serenity entered into her, and as her steps grew more bouncy and certain, so her inner chaos subsided a little.

There was a certain magic in just walking and looking around, she discovered; it was calming and healing, better than any drug. And although, once or twice, she thought of David, down in his untidy cabin, maybe sorting out the clutter of paints and brushes, or looking through the canvases that lined the walls, such thoughts were no longer painful ones. She even got to the point of telling herself, with a slight, humorous smile, that if he did decide to sack Marcus, they would at least be unemployed companions, for she was certain that her own job was in jeopardy after her outburst.

The track meandered on and suddenly she saw the gleam of sunlight on white-washed walls. The building that came into sight looked like a chapel, with a beautifully curved cupola rising up to heaven, surrounded by a natural backdrop of cypress trees. Her footsteps quickened. How interesting—a wayside chapel; if it was open she could rest there, and also have a good look around.

Outside the chapel was a small terrace with a floor of cracked paving stones. Geraniums flowered in a mass of scarlet blossom, the brilliant heads falling, haphazard, down the sides of a huge stone wine jar. Beyond, in the shady green of the surrounding trees, Annie heard bird song, and was enchanted at the solitude of the place.

She walked to the door, finding it half-open and then paused, accustoming herself to the dimness within. As she stood there, she heard a voice murmuring—not wanting to disturb someone at their devotions she drew back, uncertainly, and in that moment the faint voice said words that she could not help but overhear.

". . . Katnina, Papa . . . Annie . . . David . . ."

The English names were highlighted in the vibrant liquidity of the Greek language, and she caught her breath. By now her eyes were used to the half-light; she looked into the chapel and saw Alexa kneeling by the altar.

She knew she should tiptoe away, unseen, unheard, but some urgent need overcame the niceties of etiquette; it was suddenly vital to find out what Alexa was doing. Why should the child be here, all alone, praying for her family and two English acquaintances? Annie felt herself totally caught up in the drama of the situation and unable to leave. She felt here, in this quiet and holy place, a message awaited her—and one that only Alexa could interpret.

So she slipped into the chapel and sat down quietly on one of the hard wooden benches lining the walls, noticing Alexa's crutches cast down on the floor beside the child, as she kneeled at the foot of a plaster statue, no doubt a saint, badly needing a fresh coat of blue paint.

The saint's eyes were dull, her smile a mere crack across the oval of her pale face. Alexa, noticed Annie with deepening interest, was staring up at the cracked face, her own expression alight with adoration and hope. Annie felt she had never seen Alexa look like this—relaxed, truly childlike, and happy. Intrigued, she blatantly eavesdropped as the child's voice whispered on.

She couldn't understand all that Alexa was saying, but the names kept cropping up; Katnina, David—Papa, Annie. Annie's mind began to work overtime. What could Alexa be asking for? For asking she most certainly was; the bunch of brilliant wild flowers laid on the skirts of the statue proclaimed that. And the expression on her face, too, was one of humble petition.

The peaceful atmosphere of the chapel, combined with the warmth and the pleasant fragrance of beeswax candles, relaxed Annie so much that when, finally, Alexa finished her prayers and reached for the crutches, she was able to say, quite naturally and easily, "Let me help you, Alexa—I hope you don't mind me being here?"

The child's face was a sudden blend of surprise and dismay, slowly replaced by a growing smile. Standing up, she let Annie hand her the crutches. "How did you get here, Annie?"

"I walked—like you. Wasn't it a long journey for you, on these things?" She let Alexa precede her out into the sunshine and for a moment they stood on the paved courtyard, smiling at each other.

"Yes, but I managed. I had nothing else to do—and it was important, coming here to see the Lady."

"The—the Lady?"

"The Lady of Miracles. We always pray to her when we need." Alexa nodded very certainly, and Annie felt tenderness sweep through her. These islanders were child-like but sincere, and her worldliness, small though it was compared with David's sophistication, seemed remote and out of place in a situation such as this.

She said gently, "And you were praying?"

"Of course. For two things. First, my leg, that it may grow strong very soon. And then for . . ." Alexa turned away, her eyes clouded and a secret look enclosing her face.

"It's all right, you don't have to tell me," said Annie hastily. "Let's go back down the track, shall we? If you come to the villa with me, I'm sure David will drive you home, if Marcus isn't there."

Silently they walked for a little way, Alexa's crutches grating on the stoney path. Then, abruptly, she stopped, slipping down on the bleached grass beside the track. "I want to tell you something, Annie," she said urgently.

Annie slid down beside her. "What is it, love?"

Alexa heaved a deep sigh, and then said in a low, halting voice, "My Papa is very angry with David . . ."

202

Spontaneous laughter, bittersweet, gurgled up through Annie's thoughts. "That's funny! I thought it was David who was the angry one!"

"But why should *he* be angry?" Alexa looked alarmed.

"Because—" Annie stopped quickly. It would be heartless to say anything about Marcus's mismanagement of the business. But even as she tried to cover the awkward moment, Alexa went on solemnly, "Because my Papa does things that upset David; yes, I know it. I have heard him talking while he thinks I am asleep. He forgets to do the work for the villa visitors, and he says his accounts are all wrong— and it is all because of *me.* Oh, Annie, if he is found out, will they send him to prison?"

Annie was astounded. She caught the small, tense hand that played unthinkingly with a length of dried grass, all her feeling going out to the vulnerable child, too old for her years, and caught in a situation which preyed on her sensitive mind. But what could she say to comfort her? Alexa had spoken nothing but the truth.

"Alexa—love—you really mustn't

worry like this. You'll never get strong and healthy if you take things so much to heart. I mean . . ." Her words died away hopelessly as the little girl stared sombrely at her, dark eyes brimming with tears and mouth quivering tremulously.

"Sometimes I think I never will get strong again . . ."

"That's nonsense! Of course you will. Give yourself time. All the swimming will help; surely your leg's beginning to feel stronger already, isn't it?"

Alexa looked down at the frail leg, clearly so much weaker than the other. "Perhaps," she admitted slowly. "But it's —in *here*—that I don't feel strong, Annie . . ." Explicitly, she touched her breast, and Annie's arms went round her in a spontaneous gesture of love and understanding, willing all the anxieties and problems to resolve themselves. It was wrong that Alexa should feel like this— but what could she do to help the child?

"Oh love, don't say that. Everything will be fine, I promise you," she said stoutly, smoothing back Alexa's dark hair.

"You are sure, Annie?"

"Absolutely sure. Just believe that,

Alexa, and you'll make it happen. Positive thinking—that's what you need."

"Then if you say so, I will try. I love you, Annie . . ."

They smiled fondly at each other, and Annie felt a new determination grow within her; before she left Doloffinos she would see Alexa well on the way to full recovery and happiness, or die in the attempt. Damn David and Marcus and their ridiculous feuding . . .

"We'd better make a move home, love; let me help you up."

As they walked along the track, the quietness was abruptly broken by the sound of an approaching car. Alexa stared into the distance, her face lit by a brilliant smile. "It's Papa!"

In a few seconds the car pulled up beside them, and Marcus said querulously, "Ah, so there you are. I've been looking for you all the afternoon—until someone said they'd seen Annie coming along here, towards the chapel."

His customary smile was absent, Annie noticed. Her anxiety sprung back at once; had he and David had another row? Had he, perhaps, actually been relieved of his post?

His indignant words made her mind go blank for a second, as relief poured through her. Clearly, all he was worried about was Alexa's disappearance. "Why did you come all this way, on your own?"

"I'm sorry Papa, I only wanted to—" But he didn't seem to want to hear any more, as he turned and scowled at Annie.

"Mrs. Potter says you're going with David to her beach party on Saturday!"

Annie helped Alexa into the car. "That's right. She more or less insisted. Why, what's wrong?"

"Everything is wrong!" He crashed the gears noisily. "You can't possibly go with David—what is he thinking of? Unless he is just being polite—maybe he didn't want to appear rude. Yes, that must be it . . ."

"Wait a minute, Marcus." Annie frowned and stared at the back of his head as the car raced forward. "What are you trying to say? That David didn't really want to take me, is that it? And was too polite to say so?" A mixture of pain and annoyance swept through her; how much more could she take? It was one thing after another and no let-up.

Marcus looked over his shoulder and glared at her. "Of course he doesn't really want to take you! He has Katnina, hasn't he? They go everywhere together—so why should he ask you?"

"Oh, I give up!" Annie exploded wearily. "I just don't want to be involved any more in anything!"

His eyes widened at the anger in her voice. "No, no, Annie, don't be so cross. It's just a little misunderstanding, that's all." Ridiculously, now he was the patient one, while she felt full of hurt pride and irritation. He turned and smiled soulfully at her. "David takes Katnina," he repeated gently, "and I take you."

"And me?" asked a little voice beside him, and at once he smiled down at Alexa, reassuring and full of his usual bounce and good humour. "Of course and you, my little love! Mrs. Potter said certainly to bring you."

Annie sighed. "Well, I don't know what to think, Marcus. David definitely asked me to go—although I tried to get out of it. Mrs. Potter suggested it at first, but then he began insisting . . ."

"Don't worry, Annie! Everything is going to be lovely. You will enjoy yourself you see—a beach party by moonlight is a very special occasion. Something you will never forget—Alexa and I make sure of that, eh, my darling?"

"Yes, Papa." The smile Alexa turned on Annie was a glowing one, now that the problem had been worked out. But Annie couldn't help wondering what effect Marcus's lightning changes of mood had on the little girl; she knew that she herself was already more than exhausted by the quicksilver emotions that ran through the lifeblood of these islanders . . .

There was no sign of David for the rest of the day, and Annie was thankful to be able to spend the evening on her own after Marcus had taken Alexa home. The seething chain of confrontations that had swept her along since her arrival on Doloffinos had given her much food for thought, and so it was with immense relief that she ate her solitary supper on the darkening terrace and went to bed early, picking up a paperback from the bookcase in the hall as she went to her room.

But the traumas of fictional lives failed to hold her interest, and it was late before she was finally able to calm her restless thoughts and relax her taut body sufficiently to allow herself to sleep.

And the last conscious thought running through her mind was—*Where is David? Is he with Katnina?* Small wonder, then, that her night's rest was alive with recurring and frustrating dreams.

9

MORNING came and with it a reminder that Alexa's swimming lesson mustn't be forgotten. Annie dressed hurriedly, wondering whether she might dare to jog David's memory about it—but she needn't have worried, for his first words, when they met on the terrace for breakfast, proved that he hadn't forgotten.

"Morning Annie—ready for our swim?"

It was as if their hard words yesterday had never been said. His snappiness, followed so surprisingly by the quiet comment about her gift for understanding, had now given way to a pleasantly friendly manner. It crossed Annie's mind, with a stab of new knowledge, that maybe he hadn't been altogether wrong in hinting that he, himself, needed her understanding.

With his usual perception, he saw the faint smile touching her face. "What's so funny, then?"

"You are." She held her breath, waiting for him to pounce on her swift rejoinder, but he merely pushed the sugar bowl towards her and raised a silvery eyebrow.

"Well, being funny is far nicer than being—what were your words?—hurtful and unthinking."

She had the grace to blush. "Yes, you're right, and I'm sorry I said such beastly things."

"Don't be," he said, fixing her with such a keen glance that she fell silent at once. "I've got a feeling you're good for me, Annie—maybe I'll get you to give me some more inside information about what makes me tick. But not just now. We've got a full morning, what with Alexa's swim and then the inevitable work on the figures . . ."

"David." Marcus stood in the doorway and they both looked around sharply as his plainly upset voice cut through David's last words.

"'Morning, Marcus." David's eyes narrowed, but he kept the friendly smile on his face. "Something wrong? Don't say we're going to have another row, dear blood-brother . . ."

"No row." Marcus entered the terrace, walking across to the far wall and then turning to look back at them. "Simply getting things straight. About Mrs. Potter's beach party."

David continued nonchalantly with his breakfast. "Well, what about it?"

"Annie has misunderstood you, I think. She seems to believe she is going with *you*, but I told her no, that was a mistake. You take Katnina, as usual; Annie comes with *me*."

Marcus's emphatic words held a hint of barely controlled anger. David pushed away his plate and sat well back in his chair. He looked across at Annie, who wished she was a million miles away from the pair of them. She saw annoyance sweep across his face, watched his eyes fire into sparkling chips of ice and then, as quickly, thaw again. He was making a great effort to control himself, she thought.

"Sorry, old friend, it's you who've got it wrong," he said quietly. "Annie comes with *me*—Katnina is working, and anyway . . ." He let the unfinished words trail into the taut silence and then

212

continued in the same quiet voice. "You and Alexa will also be going—so no doubt we can make up a foursome. No . . ." His voice grew clipped and stronger as he forestalled Marcus's obvious wrath. "No, for heaven's sake don't let's make a big production scene out of this, Marcus . . ."

"But you are quite wrong!" broke out Marcus passionately, "Katnina will take the evening off! You *must* take her! It is expected—everyone knows how it is with you and Katnina . . ."

David was on his feet crossing the terrace in one swift movement before Marcus's increasingly furious words had ended.

"Shut up, Marcus. I've had enough of this. I won't have Annie subjected to such downright rudeness as you're showing. She's coming to Mrs. Potter's party as my guest, and that's final."

Marcus stood there, trembling, and Annie watched as uncontrollable anger swept across his face. Then he growled something and left the terrace with long, purposeful strides. She felt the tension leave her. "Whew! What a temper!"

David stood where he was, staring out

to sea, his voice only just reaching her. "I apologise for all that. Typical of Marcus when he can't get his own way. I told you the Greeks were an emotional lot."

"But—" She wanted to ask so many questions, the most urgent being—*does everybody know how it is with you and Katnina?* But of course, that was unthinkable; it was none of her business and she would do well to remember it. Despair once again filled her; she wished Mrs. Potter had stayed in America—how could she possibly go to the damned beach party now, with the two men snarling and snapping over her like a pair of jealous dogs?

Suddenly the idea became very funny. She started to laugh and went on and on, tears eventually running down her cheeks.

David said off-handedly, "Come to think of it, you're pretty emotional yourself . . . buck up, Annie—when you've recovered we'll go and find Alexa. If you're up to it, that is . . ."

In the soothing atmosphere of cool water and underwater fascination, Annie was able to briefly forget all the many conflicts that were making up her stay in Doloffinos. As before, she helped support Alexa, who seemed a little stronger and brighter than the previous day. When the snorkelling was finished and Alexa taken back to the beach, Annie had her usual quiet swim, her thoughts idly centred on David's gentleness with the child and the fact that he could so willingly give up his precious time to help her.

But, as she came out of the water and went slowly up the beach towards her towel, she saw that Marcus had joined Alexa and, from the look on his heavy face, was still very angry. And, quite naturally, his bad mood was reflected in Alexa's suddenly anxious expression. Annie felt indignant; didn't the stupid man realise how vulnerable his daughter was? He had no right to load his passions and worries on her frail shoulders. She was glad when Marcus stalked back to the villa and left them alone, giving her the chance to talk brightly to Alexa about the forthcoming party, and see, within minutes, a new happiness creep back into the child's face.

David came up the beach as they were getting ready to leave. He grinned down at

Alexa. "I'm not carrying you today, either you're getting too heavy or I'm losing my strength . . . see if you can manage with just an arm to help you."

Annie silently approved of this; Alexa mustn't be smothered with help, however pathetic she might appear. She watched their rather uneven progress up the beach towards the villa and heard Alexa's laughter ring out at something foolish that David had said; he could be so understanding, so family-minded, when he chose. What, she wondered, had gone wrong in his life to make him hide such warm feelings beneath that brittle, sometimes even unpleasant, facade? Would she ever know? She sighed—and then, with an immense effort of will, thought instead of getting back to work.

Annie was grateful for the afternoon interlude of rest and privacy. She knew that a long, tiring evening loomed ahead. As the afternoon slipped past she tried to force the restless thoughts into more constructive channels; perhaps, after all, the beach party in the evening would be a happy, carefree time, with none of the problems she expected. And there was one thing she was quite sure about it—Alexa was going to enjoy herself, come what may.

At tea time, when she ventured into the kitchen, she found the villa deserted. David's desk was neat and empty, the list of enquiries and complaints dealt with, and the big black-bound ledger shut. She stared at it distastefully; who would have thought that such a thing could contain dynamite . . . enough potential force, even, to separate friends of many years' standing and disrupt the life of a small child. The idea brought her worries flooding back and she had to leave the office quickly to prevent herself becoming overwrought.

I won't think about such things. I'm going to the beach party and I'm going to have fun . . . She made herself a cup of tea and then found several tasks which busied her until David returned, a little after six o'clock.

He came into the villa looking as if his mind was elsewhere, seemingly surprised to see her there. Sitting down on the desk edge he said mildly, "You're having a long day, aren't you?"

Cautiously, she looked at him. There were traces of paint on his fingers and a smudge on his shabby shorts. So he'd spent the afternoon in the cabin—unbidden and unwanted came the thought that no doubt Katnina had been there, too.

"I—I was just checking the totals again. It's easy to make mistakes, to misread Marcus's writing . . ." Her voice fell away. She hated the idea of re-opening the old wound. Anxiously she scanned David's face, waiting for him to take up where she had left off, but the expected fierceness was missing, and she felt that instead he was concentrating on her, no longer on Marcus. Uncomfortably, she tidied the papers and got up. "Have you had some tea? Shall I make you a cup?"

He didn't reply at once, and a long silence grew between them, making her aware of him as never before. Such a handsome man, with sun-touched hair and untidy clothes, who looked at her through sea-coloured eyes, assessing her, probing her innermost thoughts, almost as if she were a specimen beneath a microscope, she felt . . .

Because his intense scrutiny upset her,

and made the quick emotions of love and hopelessness swim to the surface, she withdrew behind a brittle smile and quick, easy banter.

"You'll know me again when you see me!"

"Yes . . ." He got up and came to her side; for one, heartstopping moment, she read the message in his eyes and guessed he was going to kiss her. Her body quivered and her mind blanked out; passion swept through her making her willing and full of longing. Oh, to be gathered up in his arms, to feel the beat of his heart, to taste the honey sweetness of his mouth.

But, even as her own heart pounded and she closed her eyes in glorious anticipation, he left her. At the door his voice swept back to her. "We'll leave in an hour. Bring something warm—it gets chilly at sea when the sun goes down."

Overwhelmed by shame and disappointment she heard him go to his room and knew herself rejected. With a little gasp of self-pity she escaped to the solitude of her own bedroom, and cursed Mrs. Potter for forcing her into the situation that lay ahead. She knew herself to be a mere pawn in a game, being mercilessly used by someone who cared nothing for her; for it was now quite obvious that David was only taking her to the party under protest.

In a kind of unconscious despair she showered and got ready. It was difficult to know what to wear, but that was a minor detail; no one would notice her, anyway. So she put on the pleated cotton she had bought in the village, as being suitable to the occasion—slid into heeless sandals with pretty jewelled straps between her toes, and then picked up the creamy Aran shawl that had been a present from older sister Anne-Marie last Christmas. It had a warm and cosy feel to it, and she thought then of her family back in England. When all the muddle here was finally cleared up, what heaven it would be to go home—to where security and unstinted, under-standing love awaited her. But in the meantime she must soldier on alone.

David waited on the terrace. "Ready? Good. We'll go down to the cove. Sharon always has her party in the same place, a little bay called Voolani, a few miles around the coast. She and the old boy go in their motor yacht, like most of the other guests. And there's the occasional hired caique as well." He stood at the villa door allowing her to precede him down the path, and as she passed, she saw undoubted appreciation in his eyes.

"You look gorgeous, Annie."

Momentarily her pulses raced, but by now her sense of survival was working overtime; there was no way in which she was going to let David's easy charms get the better of her again.

Off-handedly—pleased with her control—she returned his smile. "Thanks. I hope the sea won't be rough?"

"It's set fine, no fear of a storm, but there's always a wind at sea—what the islanders called the *meltemi*, the sprite of the Aegean; how does that appeal to your romantic soul?"

"Sounds most attractive—but I'm becoming quite hardened to Greek emotions by now . . ."

If he noticed the curtness of her words he gave no sign, and together they went down towards the headland. Beneath the canopy of trees the shadows were ghostly, the overhead music more haunting than Annie would have thought possible, recalling the light-hearted merriment of its morning song. She passed the dark shape of the cabin, steeling herself not to look, to ignore the open door, to forget the remembered intimacy of its dimlit interior. But even as she struggled to keep the painful thoughts away, one name echoed around her mind. *Katnina, Katnina . . .*

David's boat was swaying gently at anchor in the deeper water, several metres beyond the tideline. "Hop in." He helped her into the small dinghy that lay on its side, close to the lapping waves. With a roar the outboard motor sprang to life and they were off, racing over the water towards the larger boat.

Once aboard, with the empty dinghy trailing in their wake, Annie was again caught by the irresistible magic which had ensnared her on the first occasion she had sailed with David. The exploding waves lapped the bows as the boat thrust forward, and she felt they were breasting the depths like fabulous creatures of forgotten mythology.

Out of the cove they were slapped by the capricious wind, and Annie pulled her shawl closer. They joined a small flotilla of dinghies, cruisers and brightly painted island caiques, all heading in the same direction. From one of the boats, wafted around teasingly by the wind, came the sound of a guitar and a man's voice, resonant and beautiful.

Annie's face was cold, but as the wind caressed it she began to feel uplifted and in another world, far removed from the petty issues of everyday life. Out here it was clean and empty and marvellous; she would always remember tonight—the island drifting away behind her, mysteriously wrapped in velvety darkness, with small pinheads of light shining out from the villas dotting the headland. A heady fragrance came drifting off the land, and she recognised the sweetness of drying thyme. Gradually the music and the song ended, and there was left only the breathing silence of the sea.

Something made her turn; she stared at David, a shadowed vital figure behind her. As if he shared her thoughts he leaned forward, touching her shoulder lightly. "Enjoying yourself?"

It was a full minute before she could reply. The feel of his hand had evoked momentous sensations within her. She wanted, abruptly and desperately, to go to him, to put her arms about him and pull his head down to hers, to kiss the firm mouth that could sometimes smile so dangerously, yet at others was obstinately hard and arrogant.

It was a shocking urge that filled her, unfamiliar and frightening. Memories assailed her mockingly—his remembered voice floated around her restless mind; *When are you going to grow up, Annie?*; and she knew, with disturbing clarity that she was ready to start the process if only he, too, was willing.

The boat rolled unexpectedly. His hand left her shoulder to return to the rudder, and reality overtook her again. A little light-headed still, she answered his all-but-forgotten question.

"Yes, I am enjoying myself . . . it's absolutely glorious out here."

"I told you so, didn't I? Being at one with the water and the sunset is an experience one doesn't easily forget—but you haven't seen anything yet. How about this?"

They rounded a craggy headland, and

suddenly there was a beach ahead of them. A huge, shadowed arch of glistening marble caught the last faint tinge of sunset, and the reflection of the apricot-into-flame coloured sky lit up the waves, rolling in a creamy fichu down the length of the silver-gold sands. Annie was speechless, feeling the beauty stretched out before her to be almost unbearable.

David cut the motor and the boat lost speed, idling along in mysterious indigo depths. A long stone jetty drew nearer, and slowly the activity of voices and people overtook the serene silence of the bay.

"Driftwood," ordered someone, already ashore. "Drag it up the rocks and we'll get the fire going."

"Who's got the bucket of fish?"

"Give me a hand with these bottles . . ."

The spell of isolated enchantment was broken, and Annie discovered it was fun to join the crowd of revellers, to wade ankle-deep through the soft warm sand up to the spot where the food had been carried, and to help prepare the meal while the men of the party beach-combed for driftwood.

Alexa appeared, hopping determinedly around the rocks, looking for her. "Annie! Isn't it lovely here? Voolani is my favourite beach . . . when you swim here the marble makes it like a green painted bath."

Mrs. Potter loomed up, her expensive outfit seeming out of place amid such primitive surroundings. "Alexa, you can help me unwrap the cheeses and the tomatoes." Her face softened marginally. "My, but you're looking pretty tonight— is that a new dress, my dear?"

"Thank you—yes, Katnina made it." Alexa's wide smile expressed her appreciation of the unexpected compliment. Annie, buttering chunks of bread, watched Mrs. Potter's devouring eyes widen with instant curiosity. "Did she, indeed? How clever—but she's a talented girl, so many things she's good at . . ." The sky-blue eyes glanced down at Annie, making the seemingly innocent remark sound full of innuendo. Annie went on buttering, suddenly tense, her happiness abruptly shattered.

"And she should be here tonight— David must miss her terribly. Oh, but I'm so sorry, Miss Frayne, I didn't mean to

226

suggest that he's not enjoying having *you* here instead . . ."

A dark shadow fell over them, and Marcus interrupted the spiteful voice. "Katnina was sorry not to come, Mrs. Potter, but of course she meets David at other times. They are always together, as they always have been."

"Of course," cooed Mrs. Potter, smiling up at him with practised charm. "Why, we all know how close they are, the two dear things!"

Annie watched Mrs. Potter's quick mind echoing her own thoughts; that Marcus's clumsy excuses did no more than emphasise the fact that David and Katnina were not here together this evening and that David had brought another girl in her place.

The old resentment smouldered anew, and she felt her hands tremble as she went on automatically helping to prepare the picnic. She wished that Marcus would stop being so insistent in his excuses, or that Mrs. Potter would go and talk to her other guests, but no, Marcus's heavy voice went on and on, still trying to explain things to his own advantage.

227

"After all, David is Annie's boss, and so it was only polite he should invite her in his boat—but in real truth she is here with *me*. Oh, and Alexa, of course . . ."

But Mrs. Potter had gleaned all she needed. Already she had turned her ample back on them, her corncrake voice calling to other friends—no doubt, imagined Annie angrily, to spread the news that the little English girl was making trouble between Marcus and David, and wasn't it a shame about poor dear Katnina?

It was a huge relief, then, to see David lugging an enormous bleached piece of sprawling driftwood up to the already crackling bonfire. Annie got up, avoided Marcus's persistent presence, and ran to where Alexa sat, deep in conversation with one of the villa guests who hadn't heard about the accident, and who was clearly engrossed in the sad story. Seeing the child in congenial company, and not needing her, Annie looked around, wondering vaguely where she might escape to.

"You've done your bit, so come over here and let's find somewhere quiet to sit." David's touch, his vibrant voice, and the demand in his shadowed eyes silenced the angry words clamouring in her head, and she followed him obediently. He found a rock, set a little apart, and pulled her down beside him, wryly dusting the moonlit sand before her skirt touched it.

"You look out of this world tonight, Annie. I hardly recognise you as the girl who snapped my head off within minutes of our first meeting."

Anxiously, she listened for the familiar ring of mockery, but there was none. She looked at him through the twilight and he smiled reassuringly, as if he knew how she felt. "I'll get us something to eat. Now, stay there . . ."

The words held such command that she wouldn't have been able to move, even had she wanted to do so. But tonight she felt that her usually quick resilience was lowered, that all she wanted was for him to return, to sit close enough for her to touch, to talk to her in that comfortable, gentle way in which he sometimes spoke to Alexa, yet so seldom to her.

She sensed that the ruthless man of international business fame had disappeared; closing her eyes, she attempted to control her fermenting emotions, but to no avail. The evening was affecting her in a strange, sensuous way. She knew she would make the most of his company tonight, for tomorrow he would again be different; this—*this*—was the David she preferred, the David she could so easily allow herself to love.

He was back before she could come to terms with the incredible truth of her thoughts and she edged away, taking the laden plate he offered, and then urgently trying to control herself while he went off to get some wine.

When he returned again, she was calmer, even though, beneath her still surface, elation and doubt bubbled alarmingly. David slid down beside her. "Everything to Madam's liking, I hope?"

She looked at the colourful salad and the little, sizzling fish which had been cooked on sticks over the salty, driftwood fire. A tiny smile lifted her mouth as she glanced up at his watching face. Everything was, indeed, to her liking; particularly the man himself, so close to her in the moonlight.

"Very much so, thank you." But how much he would never know, for she would never dare tell him. She ate with no hunger, only an urgent need to keep her thoughts and sensations at bay.

He held his glass towards her. "Who shall we drink to, Annie?" His voice was soft and personal in the quietness that held them apart from the other revellers, spread out in small intimate groups along the silvery beach.

Her heart quickened, but she said primly, "To—to Alexa, of course. To her complete and quick recovery."

For a long moment he held her glance and she knew instinctively that he was amused at her cowardice. But he nodded and repeated after her—"To Alexa."

They touched glasses and drank, her mind full of joy and yet alive with a warning that tried hard to undermine the happiness. She looked into his eyes and knew that he had forgotten Alexa, forgotten everything except her nearness and the magic potency of the evening. She was sufficiently experienced, in her own innocent way, to recognise the intent of every warm-blooded man on a moonlit night.

Turning her head away from his compelling stare, she made herself hang on to reality. Then someone passed them, bare feet scuffing the sand and a friendly voice shouting a greeting. She was thankful, yet angry, at the respite. Could she keep him at bay for the rest of the evening? Did she truly want to avoid what, she knew deep inside her, would be a passionate and sensual experience? Even as desire and caution battled in her mind David's hand gently began stroking her arm, sending tingles through her tense body.

"I want to ask you something," he said as the evening shadows intensified and music struck up further down the beach.

"Y—yes?" She didn't dare look at him. But the sweet sensation of his stroking fingers was fast working an enchantment. If she didn't get away soon—now—this minute—she would be lost. "Yes?" she whispered again, her voice a mere breath against the throbbing guitar.

"Look at me, Annie." There was no refusing the familiar tone of command and obediently she turned her face towards him.

"Can we arrange a truce?" he asked, docilely enough, but with a quirk of his mobile mouth, and she saw the humour in his deep eyes. "You're such a different girl tonight, I'm a bit scared."

"Don't laugh at me," she pleaded, not caring if he perceived the seriousness of her mood.

"Who's laughing? That gorgeous dress, this meek and mild creature who hasn't answered me back once the whole evening —is this the new Annie Frayne? Or maybe an older one I hadn't got around to discovering before . . ."

"It's still me," she said honestly. "And if you really want a truce—well, all right. I mean, I never wanted to fight in the first place; not until you started being so aggressive and rude and . . ." Just in time she saw a flicker of fire spark in his watching eyes and stopped herself.

They looked at each other for a long moment, and then laughed.

"See what I mean? We're both so quick to anger . . . I definitely need a signed truce if I'm going to spend the rest of the night with you!" His hand reached out across her, and one long finger printed words in the pale sand next to her. Annie looked down to see what he was writing.

Laughing, she signed her name and then caught her breath as his hands captured hers. His face was very near and she could smell the salt of the sea water on his damp hair. "You're slipping," he whispered wryly, "you failed to pick me up on a vital, controversial point."

Totally bemused, Annie's heart raced. "I did?" she murmured helplessly. "The music's so loud I must have missed it— what did you say?"

"Merely suggested that we spend the rest of the night together." He watched her through the growing darkness, still imprisoning her hands.

Annie knew she was caught. Danger sparked all around her; the moonlight, the intimacy of the long shadows, the lulling song of guitar and sea . . . who was she to resist it? And yet, a built-in alarm system was still in action. What a fool she was to fall for this island romance stuff; as the thought hit her she tried to free her hands, but David held them fast.

"Stop it," he said light-heartedly. "Do as you're told. Remember I'm your boss . . ." He pulled her gently to him and she felt the warmth of his body against hers, his lips, like moths in the moonlight, bringing her delighted senses to a heady climax.

And then a rough voice shattered the spell.

"Annie!" growled Marcus, appearing like a thunderstorm out of the darkness, "You're meant to be with me—had you forgotten?"

10

DAVID was on his feet instantly, and she sat there, frozen with horror, watching the two men as they faced each other.

"For God's sake Marcus, control yourself!" She heard the flaring anger in David's voice and put her head in her hands, only half-believing what was happening. But there was to be no escape from the ugly confrontation.

Marcus glared into David's eyes. "You have no right to make love to her, you're Katnina's lover!" he hissed in a low, furious voice. "She adores you, waits for you to speak . . . David, you're a bastard! I have to teach you a lesson!"

There was a still, taut moment of silence and Annie heard the quickening breaths as they took stock of each other. She sensed too well what they were thinking—Marcus yearning for a fight to bring his over-brimming emotions to a head, and David, equally passionate yet with a tighter control of himself, ready to stall, to talk things over rather than resort to blows.

In that moment of agonising anticipation, she leaped to her feet and fled, racing away down the beach with a shuddering sense of panic, wanting only to get away from the fearfulness behind her. Intent on their own business, neither man saw her go.

As she ran onto the stone jetty, she heard Mrs. Potter arranging for one of the hired caiques to return to the village. ". . . another crate of retsina, I think . . ."

"I'd like to go with him," said Annie hurriedly, trying to hide her emotional state. "I've got a headache . . ." It was only the whitest of lies, for in truth by now there was a heavy band of pain pressing over her eyes and she yearned for the comfort of her bedroom back at the villa.

"You poor dear! But who'll go with you? Where's that naughty David gone?" Mrs. Potter's eyes ranged the length of the darkened beach, and Annie prayed desperately that she wouldn't see the sparring figures behind the rocks.

"I don't need anyone with me, Mrs.

Potter. Please don't spoil his evening—or Marcus's . . ." She wanted suddenly to laugh at the falsity of what she was saying; more urgently still she repeated her words. "I'll be all right on my own, truly—"

"Well, if you're quite sure?"

The boatman was elderly and smiled understandingly as she climbed aboard the swaying caique. The craft swung around and headed out into the open sea, and the cool wind stung her face, whipping her shoulders and bare arms painfully, making her realise that there was, indeed, no escape from the realities of life, however hard one shrank from experiencing them.

She wondered bleakly what she had left behind her on the beach; whether even now the enmity that had been slowly but surely building up between David and Marcus had worked itself out. And who the victor might be . . .

Annie was weeping silently as the boat moored at Doloffinos waterfront, and it was with utter weariness and despair that she sought a taxi, to drive her back to the villa. Much, much later, lying sleepless in her silent room, she heard sounds of returning revellers; a car started up, and she thought Alexa said something in her shrill voice. And there were footsteps in the hallway of the villa, quiet footsteps that approached her door and paused.

She froze, unable to decide what to do; then they went away and seconds later a door closed and she knew that David had decided against rousing her. It was a long time before she slept.

Next morning she was alone in the office. David, so Anthula told her brightly, had risen early and gone down to the headland. Maybe he was out in his boat. And Marcus hadn't arrived yet. Annie heaved a sigh of relief even as she called herself an arrant coward. Eventually she would have to face finding out what had happened last night at Voolani.

So she plodded on with her task, which was an unpleasant one; David had left a note on the desk asking her to list all of Marcus's incorrect entries in the ledger. Her heart sank as she began to do so. Was there to be still more anger, further confrontations?

Just before lunch she took a telephone call from the firm of accountants in Athens who were auditing the books. The message was briefly to the point; discrepancies to the value of just over fifteen hundred pounds had been found, and before the audit could be completed Mr. Nicholas must instruct them as to how the accounts were to be reconciled—where was the repayment of £1,500 to come from? Perhaps he would phone back, at his earliest convenience.

Annie replaced the receiver with hands that were suddenly moist with chill perspiration. So this was it—the moment she had been dreading ever since the unhappy situation of embezzlement became clear. She knew she had to find David and give him the message—and at the same time learn just what had happened last night.

The midday sun beat down with a force that made her blink as she left the villa, heading down the track towards the headland. Beneath the whispering trees she sighed with relief as the shade enveloped her. Quickly she walked down to the cabin. For once the music in the pine tops didn't register—her mind was too fully occupied to listen for it.

What if David was out in his boat? She half-hoped he was—at least it would delay the moment she dreaded. But her heart sank when she saw the dinghy moored at the water's edge and the bigger boat riding the swell further out in the bay. So he must be there, in the cabin—painting, maybe.

On the threshold she hesitated, then, taking her courage up anew, rapped on the open, weather-bleached door and heard her voice crack uncertainly as she called his name. "David—are you there?"

For a moment there was no sound, then she heard soft movement. Taking a few steps into the cabin she stared around.

"Hallo, Annie." He was leaning a canvas against the far wall, glancing back over his shoulder at her as he did so. He looked preoccupied, and she wished wretchedly that she had a less onerous message to give him. Anxious to get it over quickly, she said, "The accountants phoned and want a decision from you; I came down at once. Anthula said you might be here."

He padded across the floor, feet bare, dressed only in the faded, shabby denim shorts. His hands, she noticed automatically, were stained with paint, and there was a speck on his right cheek.

Face to face with her, he stood quite still, his eyes a translucent green in the shadowy room. From deep down inside her, words forced themselves out. "David —what happened last night? It was so awful . . . and all my fault . . ."

He touched her cheek without replying and her heart felt it must explode with the intensity of her emotions. Then his expression relaxed slightly and he smiled at her. "It's all right, don't worry about it. Nothing happened."

"N—nothing? But—"

"I told Marcus not to be a fool. Too much wine, seeing you beside me, the moonlight . . . you mustn't take the blame, Annie, it was all a big blow-up of those famous Greek emotions."

She stared, unable to believe the anti-climax. "But what he said about Katnina —and you—?"

David's smile shifted imperceptibly and he turned away, going over to a corner cupboard and opening it. "All part of the build-up. Marcus has always been ferociously possessive in his relationships.

He doesn't change as he gets older. Like a drink? You look rather hot and bothered . . ."

Lost in her confused thoughts, she watched him produce glasses and tins of Coke from the cupboard. He came back and nodded towards the couch. "Sit down —the only accommodation I can offer, I'm afraid. But it has the reputation of being fairly comfortable."

She heard the familiar light note of mockery and wondered at it. Sitting down on the very edge of the couch she sipped her drink and tried to regain her self-control. But the added anxiety of the phonecall, and the knowledge that very soon there was bound to be a final explosion between him and Marcus, combined with the undoubted magnetism of David's presence beside her, put an end to such efforts.

Undeniably weak and susceptible, she was overcome with the certain knowledge that if David as much as smiled at her now she would simply fall at his feet, submitting to whatever mastery he chose to claim over her.

A wasp droned crossly against the

window, and a sudden acceleration of wind from the sea aroused the nearby pines to sing louder and more evocatively. Annie's breath was shallow and her heart raced. She sought for harmless words that would break the extended silence, but her mind remained a nervous blank.

"Wind's blowing up. We're in for a storm. You'll enjoy that, Annie."

"Why—why should I?" Of all things, she hadn't quite expected a weather forecast.

"A girl like you, all fire and passion— just the one to appreciate seeing the elements at play. We're safe enough here with the door and the shutters barred. You don't have to worry, I'll look after you."

Something in his deep, quiet voice brought her head around to stare into his watching eyes. What she saw there unnerved her even further. She moved quickly, getting to her feet, for she knew she must go, now, while she was still safe. But a hand on her wrist pulled her down again. The Coke fell to the floor, neither of them noticing it. Carefully David got rid of his own glass, still holding her wrist in his strong grasp.

"You're not going anywhere Annie, so don't bother to try. This is the moment I've been waiting for—you and me alone, with the chance of really getting to know each other."

"But—the phonecall . . ."

"Damn the phonecall. It's not important." His eyes held hers, making her feel completely unable to withstand his dominance.

"Of course it's important!" she whispered, hardly knowing what she was saying. "You have to decide about Marcus, once and for all . . ."

"Marcus can wait. You and I can't. No Annie—" as she began to struggle in a last burst of near-panic, "Please don't leave me—"

"Don't—*leave you?*"

The unexpected plea kept her still, all tension suddenly fled, and a new intuitive feeling swept through her.

He smiled sadly and she thought she'd never seen him so naked, so truly himself. "Please don't," he repeated. "You see, I'm a lonely man. I have few friends and so, when I find someone like you, with a special gift of warmth and understanding,

I want to cement our friendship—strengthen it, make it last." Releasing her hand, his smile widened. She recognised the wry note of humour as he added, "I suppose you think this is just a new line in seduction?"

Annie took a deep breath and rubbed her wrist where his fingers had pressed too hard. She was free. She had only to run to the open door and leave—but perversely, now the chance was here, she had no wish to take it. David's words had intrigued her, delighted her; she knew she had to stay and hear him out.

Smiling hesitantly, hardly able to believe what he had said, she murmured, "Well, if it is, I prefer it to your last attempt."

A glow came into the eyes watching her so closely. "So I can go on?"

"Please . . ." Her whisper increased his smile. Suddenly he was on his feet, going to the door and latching it, closing the shutters of the big open window so that the only light came from a small circular pane high in the wall above the line of canvases.

"Annie—" Back at her side he looked a little anxiously into her wide eyes.

"Annie?" Touching her cheek he leaned closer. She saw humour flash across his face. "I'm almost scared to try and kiss you—are you quite sure you won't shout at me and run off?"

"Quite sure." She had never been so sure of anything in her life. All she wanted was to feel the pressure of his lips, the security of his arms about her, their two bodies warm and united on the voluptuous bed. With slow deliberation she dared to take his face between her hands and drew it towards her. Then she kissed him.

For a second he remained passive, suffering her gentle lips to find his, and then, suddenly, he was kissing her as she'd never been kissed before, the fire of his passion igniting her own until they were lying together among the cushions and pillows of the couch, lost in the sensations that engulfed them.

Annie's joy knew no bounds. She loved him, and so the ecstasy of feeling him share this wonderful moment over-shadowed any pangs of conscience that would otherwise have hit her. She knew that in a moment she must submit to him completely; her body could no longer hold out against the sensuous delight of his caresses.

"David—oh, David . . ."

He silenced her, his mouth hardening, even as his gentle hands began undoing the buttons of her dress.

She heard, as if in another world, the song of the pine trees outside as the mounting wind urged them into louder response, and thought dreamily that the music was like the blood in her veins, mounting to a climax that would be all beauty and joy. And then she heard a banging at the door, and voices shouting.

"David! Open up can't you? I've brought Katnina to see you. We have to talk. *David* . . ."

"God!"

He rolled away, face like thunder, and Annie sat up, watching as he went and slammed open the door.

"What in hell's name do you want, Marcus? Can't it wait?"

"No, it can't! Not a minute longer." Marcus strode into the cabin, pulling an unwilling Katnina with him. Annie, sitting stiffly on the edge of the couch, caught a glimpse of Alexa's frightened face in the doorway.

Katnina slapped at Marcus's hand on her arm. "Let me go! You have no right to drag me here, I want no more to do with it . . ."

"You'll do as I say!" Marcus's voice was fraught with passion as he shouted back at her. "I'm the man of the family, so stop arguing!" Abruptly, he turned and stared across the room to where David stood by the half-open door. "Now we talk! At last! No more putting it off, like you did last night, my friend . . ."

David's face set in cold disapproval, and Annie shivered. Here, at last, was the scene she had been waiting for; the scene that had come at the most inopportune moment possible. A few seconds more, and she and David would have been making love and she would have been irredeemably lost. Perhaps after all, she decided wretchedly, yet with a cynical acceptance that was entirely new to her usual pattern of thoughts, she should really be thankful that Marcus had chosen to arrive now.

"Okay, Marcus, so we'll talk. As you

say, we've been putting it off for days. I don't know just what Katnina has to do with it—or Annie either—but as they're here, they can listen."

Annie watched Katnina move slowly towards the couch, her lovely face pale and miserable. As she approached, their eyes met. Katnina looked at her almost pleadingly, and Annie put out a shaking hand. "Come and sit down."

Marcus and David faced each other across the room; then, abruptly, Marcus marched over to the table where the litter of paints and brushes stood, hammering the boards until everything jumped about. "You have spoiled it all! You change your mind, choose the wrong girl . . . why couldn't you marry Katnina? My plan would have worked that way!

"Marry Katnina?"

The amazement in David's voice sent a stab of joy through Annie; reacting quickly, she glanced at Katnina beside her, afraid what she might see on the woman's face. But Katnina was shaking her head, a slow fire beginning to burn in her fine eyes. Annie wondered—and went on listening as David said, "You're out of your mind, Marcus—there was never any question of Katnina and I marrying."

"But you are always friends! And lovers, since last year . . ."

"But no longer." David's determined words cut across Marcus's growling, insidious words and silenced him. Then David smiled, and he went over to put a hand on Marcus's shoulder. "I'm sorry, old friend—I seduced your sister, and I'm not doing the gentlemanly thing by marrying her—is that what this is all about?"

Marcus shrugged himself away. "Of course not! I'm a man of the world and you're not the only one to take a mistress when you want . . . no, no, it's more than that. It's the money, you see; the accounts that I've—what is your word? ah, *fiddled* —yes, the money that I've fiddled. I thought that if you married Katnina we could hide it, keep it in the family. After all, I don't want to find myself in gaol, do I? So, with your wedding you would be one of us and you, too, would see the sense of safeguarding the family name. That's what I thought, David . . . do you blame me?" Marcus stared hard at his friend and

Annie held her breath, wondering what on earth David's reaction to such fantasy might be. But David seemed impassive, merely listening to what was coming next.

Marcus heaved a dramatic sigh and hunched his shoulders. "But no, you spoil the whole thing. You make it obvious you don't want to marry her, and so I must be held responsible for the money; I *could* go to goal, after all . . ."

"You certainly could, Marcus," David nodded slowly. Annie could see he was thinking hard, masking his inner thoughts as he did so. Fascinated by the drama unfolding before her, she ignored the slight sound in the doorway, forgetting it immediately as Marcus started bellowing again, his voice filling the cabin with passion.

"And you would *let* me go? But we are blood-brothers—we are close, David, always have been, even as small boys . . ."

David's jaw set obstinately. "But not close enough for you to confide in me with your troubles, eh, Marcus? Surely you must have known I would help in any way I could if you were in need? If you wanted money for Alexa, why didn't you ask? It was for her treatment you took it, I suppose?"

Marcus nodded, momentarily silenced. Inside Annie's mind a shaft of light beamed down; now she understood a little more about David's moods; *a lonely man*, he had told her, but this confrontation with Marcus was revealing a vulnerability she would never have believed possible. It was becoming clear that David had been deeply wounded by Marcus's unconfiding attitude; it wasn't the money that mattered, but the lack of trust displayed by one who called himself a friend—blood-brother, even. Warmth began to creep back into her chilled body, and with the new understanding her love for him grew even deeper.

"I would have given you whatever you needed, Marcus. So why, in God's name, didn't you ask me?"

"You weren't here . . ."

"Don't be a damn fool! A letter would have reached me or a phonecall."

Katnina got to her feet, still trembling, her voice uneven and husky. "Marcus likes to play God with his family, David; he didn't ask you because he wanted to have that power over you—to force you to marry me. He has a feud against Niko's family—and I love Niko, but I am forbidden to marry him. Marcus said no when Niko offered for me and then thought up this plan—that you and I should marry . . . and I have been so unhappy over it. Forgive me, David, for my part in it all . . ."

David came across and took her in his arms, smiling down into the brimming eyes. "Lovely Katnina—there's nothing to forgive. And I'm delighted to know that you and Niko are going to be married—he's a splendid fellow—I hope you'll both be as happy as you deserve to be. Bless you, my love." He kissed her gently on both cheeks, before looking back at Marcus, one arm still around Katnina's shoulders. "All right, I admit that in a way I've been as much to blame as you, Marcus. You depended on our long friendship and I didn't trust you enough; I was angry, very angry—but even so, *you* didn't trust me, either. As you've told me so often, you and I are sworn blood-brothers Marcus—remember the blood we mingled in that highly dramatic ritual on

Voolani, once? But we're both guilty of breaking that bond—so what do we do?"

Marcus took a deep breath, then let it out slowly, glowering sulkily across the room as he did so. "So I think we must fight it out. Come outside then, David, let's get it over—and no talking me out of it, as you did last night."

A gust of wind slammed the door wide open and with the noise Annie's mind darted back to the sound she had heard only minutes ago. She stared, expecting to see Alexa still standing there, but the doorway was empty and suddenly, above the rising wind, she heard the unmistakable putt-putt of the dinghy's outboard motor. Instinct told her with alarming certainty where Alexa was.

"David—Marcus—it's Alexa!" she screamed, jerking to her feet. "She's taken the boat out—she must have heard all that you said—about Marcus going to gaol, that the money was spent on her operation —oh, God, she thinks she's to blame for everything! And now she's gone . . ."

For a fleeting moment both men seemed turned to stone, staring at her with disbelief, then, together, they both rushed out of the cabin. Annie tore after them, her one instinct to save Alexa from whatever she planned to do.

At the edge of the wind-whipped sea she paused only long enough to rip off her dress and fling away her shoes, following Marcus and David as they waded into the surf, swimming strongly out to the yacht, which leaped and jumped now in the unsheltered water beyond the curve of the bay.

Buffetted and breathless, she swam gamely in their wake and was thankful when David turned and waited for her, bearing her up and shouting in her ear, "You little fool—you shouldn't have come . . ."

"I'm—I'm all right. I'm nearly—as good as you, remember?" How could she possibly joke, she wondered vaguely, swallowing mouthfuls of water as wave after wave pounded her down. But beneath the fear and the discomfort a sliver of wonderful truth remained in her bewildered thoughts—that David no longer loved Katnina. It was treasure enough to brave a hundred oceans for, even though, at the same moment she accepted the painful fact that he could never return her own love; when all was said and done, he was still the same David, the man who took pleasure when and wherever it was offered.

Marcus reached the boat first and pulled Annie aboard. She lay on the wet boards recovering her breath while David got the engine going. As the boat trembled and then leaped forward she went to join him in the little cabin.

"Why did she do it, Annie?" David's narrowed eyes swept the turbulent waters ahead.

"Because she's been worrying for so long about Marcus taking the money; because she's afraid of violence and the idea of his going to prison. And I think she knew that Katnina really wants to marry Niko and not you. And mostly because she considered the whole thing *her* fault . . . poor little Alexa. Oh God, David, we must find her—"

"We're doing all we can. Go and talk to Marcus. He must be in a bad way."

Marcus stood in the prow of the boat, hunched like a figurehead, taking no notice of the spray or the wind. Annie dared to put a hand on his wet arm. "Don't worry, Marcus, we'll find her, of course we will . . ."

He didn't even look around, might not have heard her; he appeared torn asunder with guilt and despair, Annie thought pityingly, and she knew that no words could comfort him. Pulling around her an old jacket she found rolled up beneath a folded sail, she joined him in his silent search.

The storm grew worse, the waters heaving as if in agony. Lost in her thoughts, she was suddenly returned to reality as he roared in her ear, "There she is! By the rock—by the Black Handkerchief . . ." Clambering onto the side of the boat, he poised himself for a second and then dived, disappearing immediately in the froth of waves that tore over the menace of the hidden reef.

Annie screamed. "David—David!" Turning, she watched him lock the rudder and throw the anchor overboard, before-joining her in the prow. "Don't panic," he said firmly. "Marcus knows what he's doing. He's not a fool in the water—and he knows this coastline. Looks as if the dinghy hit the rock and capsized. Keep your eyes skinned, Annie, she must be here somewhere."

Marcus's head bobbed up, sleek as a seal, and his voice caught the noisy wind as it tore alongside the boat. "She's here —throw me the lifebelt, David—I'm going down again, her leg's stuck . . ." He went into the frothing water and for a long, terrible moment there was no sign of him.

David heaved a lifebelt over the side, secured the end of the rope and said tersely, "I'm going in. Get blankets from the cabin locker, Annie, and wrap her in them as soon as I get her aboard."

"Be careful—!" But he was gone, lost, like Marcus, in the heavy swell of breaking waves. She counted the moments in torment until his head surfaced again, shouting with relief as she saw the limp bundle supported by the lifebelt, which he towed to the side of the boat. "Alexa—oh, thank God!"

David's arms pushed the child aboard. She fell at Annie's feet, half-drowned and shivering, colourless face slowly breaking into the vestige of a smile as she realised where she was.

Wrapping the child in blankets, comforting her and seeing the colour return to the drained cheeks, Annie pushed away the fearsome dread about Marcus's safety; one thing at a time, she told herself numbly. Alexa was safe. David would rescue Marcus. There was nothing she could do but care for Alexa.

It seemed hours, but was, in fact, only minutes before voices sounded over the roar of the storm, and the boat listed heavily to one side as David heaved an unconscious Marcus aboard. He pulled the inert body out of the wind and covered it with a blanket. Annie crept from the cabin, hardly daring to ask the question that haunted her.

"Is he—is he all right?"

David wiped the water from his streaming face. "He will be. Took a crack on the head, but he'll recover. Tough as nails, these island boys. Go and get the brandy, Annie, that'll bring him back to life."

When she returned, Marcus was already coming round, his eyes focusing with sudden dread and his voice strengthening rapidly as he muttered, "Alexa? Alexa?"

"Safely aboard," David said firmly. "Like you, a bit the worse for wear, but Father Poseidon bore you both up on his broad bosom and you'll live to tell the tale of how you beat the Black Handkerchief . . . another folkstory, if I'm not mistaken." His smile was infectious and Annie watched with mounting relief as Marcus slowly smiled back at his rescuer.

"So you saved my life, David—and Alexa, too . . . we're blood-brothers again, eh? No more misunderstandings? No more rows?"

"That's about it, Marcus." They stared at each other, savouring the moment of reconciliation. Then David added jokily, "And there's no need to swig *all* my brandy—if you're okay I'll turn about and get us home."

In the cabin he smiled encouragingly at Alexa. "No more pinching my dinghy until you learn how to navigate properly, young lady. It's okay, Alexa, my darling, everything's fine now. I'll have you home in no time. Tell her a story or something Annie, to pass the time . . ."

Alexa's great brown eyes began to swim with tears. "I couldn't help it, Annie. I

261

had to do it. I was listening all the time while you were in the cabin. I heard about Papa going to gaol, about he and David fighting—suddenly I knew it was all my fault and so I ran—I took the boat, tried to get away where I wouldn't be a trouble any more."

Annie laid her cheek against Alexa's wet one. Huskily, she said, "I understand, love. But you were wrong—nothing is ever so bad that it can't be mended. Thank goodness you're safe. And we'll see that all the troubles are cleared up. You won't have to worry about anything, ever again, I promise."

A shadow blocked the light from the entrance and Marcus said quietly, "My little love, can you ever forgive me? What was I thinking of not to notice you were so upset . . . poh, poh, poh, I am a bad man, indeed."

Annie joined David at the wheel. For a moment she watched the black, rolling waters ahead with an inward shudder, remembering all too clearly how Marcus had warned her that the sea could be a monster; now she knew the truth of those words. The emotions she had so firmly held back during the last hour or so suddenly overbrimmed. "Thank God you're all safe—"

Her voice broke and David's arm gripped her shoulder. "Amen to that, Annie."

He brought the boat into the cove as near to the tideline as possible. Katnina waited there, her face breaking into a glow of relief when she saw Alexa in Marcus's arms. David jumped over the side and helped Marcus wade through the surf with his precious burden, then he returned to the boat for Annie, picking her up as if she, too, was a child, and bringing her safe to land.

For those few moments, feeling his arms warm and strong about her, hearing the steady beat of his heart so close to her ear, Annie knew a wonderful sensation of unselfish happiness. For the problems and conflicts which had raged so disastrously around them all, must surely now be ended. It was as if the sea itself had put paid to the ridiculous posturings of the puny mortals who lived alongside it . . . she smiled as David carefully lowered her feet to the beach and said gently, "Go up to the cabin, Annie—get warm and dry while I make a hot drink. I think we can all relax now."

She watched him put an arm around Katnina and hug the girl to him, comforting, encouraging her. Crunching up the beach, shivering with cold and reaction, Annie followed Marcus as he strode into the cabin and laid Alexa on the couch, tucking blankets around her, seemingly unable to take his eyes off the child's face, which was at last happy and free from secret anxiety.

Annie felt tears brimming her eyelids and hurriedly did as David had told her. Warm and dry again, she accepted the mug of coffee put into her hands and watched the little scene of reconciliation that took place between the two men.

As David offered the mug to Marcus, Annie saw a rapid interplay of emotions flood his face—irony, a fleeting moment of pain, and then a slow smile of relief and pleasure. He clasped Marcus's hand and put both arms around him in the familiar embrace. "Just like old times again, eh, Marcus? No more bad feelings."

"Ah, David, my heart is too full to

speak—you're right, of course you are. How foolish I've been . . ."

For a long moment they stared at each other, and then Alexa's small voice broke into the stretching silence. "And I shall get strong again now, Papa—now that all the trouble is over. You and David are friends again, and Katnina will marry Niko, I think . . ."

Marcus nodded tenderly and Katnina went running to his side.

"Thank you; oh, thank you, Marcus!" Turning, she looked back at David, and Annie watched her lovely face glow with blossoming happiness. "You will come to Niko's and my wedding, David—yes?"

"With the greatest possible pleasure, Katnina, love." He smiled down at her and drew her into his arms.

Annie felt her heart must burst. First of all the storm and the terrible moments when she feared first Alexa was lost and then Marcus, as well—and now this . . .

David and Katnina stood below the huge portrait that dominated the cabin, and even though she knew now that they were no more than good friends, the knowledge merely emphasised her own certainty that she herself was just one more plaything in David's lonely, sophisticated and far-removed world.

Hardly able to hold back any longer the tears that threatened, she slipped quietly from the room, unnoticed in the happiness that bound Marcus so close to Alexa, and Katnina to David's friendship; quickly she ran back to the villa, to pack her bag, and go.

11

IT took only minutes to gather her belongings and leave. She went down the path towards the cement road as the wind lowered and a watery sun again crept from behind the massed, racing clouds.

She discovered, amid the tumultuous emotions that racked her, one small true feeling—that she was doing the right thing, no matter how painful it was. However much she loved David—and she did, oh yes, she did—it wasn't enough to be just one more romantic interlude in his life.

Honestly she told herself that she would always recall with longing, and a tinge of regret, the unfinished love scenes between them; yet more pleasure must give way to her own sense of right and wrong, and she knew now that she needed marriage and a true, lasting love, if her life was to be really happy. A holiday affair, however glorious and light-hearted, was not for her.

It was all too clearly obvious that she wasn't David's sort of girl—and never would be.

At this point she had to sit down on the verge of the road and recover her strength. It had been a gruelling morning, and now that the sun was once again beaming down it was too hot to walk far with a heavy and cumbersome bag. For the first time she began to make plans. Once she reached the village she would book her passage on the ferry; thank goodness she hadn't spent all her holiday money. Perhaps it might even be possible to fly back to the mainland . . . immersed in thought she started walking again.

The village bus passed her, going the wrong way, its cloud of fumey dust making her step aside and shut her eyes. In the rumbling of its passing she was unaware of another vehicle approaching.

Suddenly a door slammed and a hand pulled roughly at her arm, making her drop the bag and look around, startled.

"And where do you think you're going?" David's face was stern and troubled, his voice vibrant with displeasure; she thought, too, she saw a look of anxiety. Weakly she tried to escape his piercing stare.

"I'm leaving. Let me go, David, *please* . . ."

"No." He swept her off her feet, carrying her back to the car as if she was weightless and dumping her without ceremony in the passenger seat. He went back for the bag and then, turning the car with a wild squeal of tyres, headed back towards the villa.

Annie felt that all her willpower had gone. She knew now what it must be like to be kidnapped, to be forced into a situation that held no possibility of release at the end of it. David, in this angry, powerflul mood, was altogether too much for her. So she sat beside him, resolve gone, waiting like a sacrificial victim for the sword to fall.

He parked the car below the villa and came around to open her door, no smile on his set face. "Out you get."

Like a sleepwalker, she allowed him to pull her up. Strangely, now that the brief but wild storm had passed, the day was beautiful again. A tear of sheer self-pity ran down Annie's cheek. How could the world go on being so lovely, when her own life was running into a brick wall?

The cabin was sitting in a burst of mid-afternoon sun, looking as shabby and neglected as she remembered. And yet—she paused instinctively, as they came out of the pine trees and David's grip on her arm grew less restrictive—there was something friendly about the little building; an invitation almost . . .

Again she was picked up, swept into his arms in a wilfully uncompromising manner. She heard his heart beat beneath the thin cotton of his shirt, felt the easy strength of the muscles that supported her and, unbelievably, knew no more fear. She belonged here in his arms, in the cabin.

He laid her on the couch, the anger gone from his face and the old, familiar, elusive tenderness tugging at her heart, recalling magical moments between them that must never be repeated.

She made a small, unwilling, last attempt to escape him, "Please don't . . . please let me go . . ." and watched the light in his sea-green eyes grow deeper and more urgent as he answered.

"Never again, Annie Frayne. I've got you for keeps this time."

The mockery didn't frighten her any longer; she felt relaxed and almost happy, despite her precarious situation. Sitting up, she sniffed the air, feeling an instinctive need to find out what had happened after she left the cabin, earlier. There was cigar smoke and a clutter of empty coffee mugs and half a bottle of brandy; so they must have sat here talking, friendly and relaxed. She hoped that all the problems had been sorted out, once and for all.

Beside her on the couch, David sat and watched—and waited. She looked around again; what was it that was different? With a gasp of realisation, she saw that Katnina's huge portrait had gone. In its place, smiling a little hesitantly down at the figures on the big couch below, hung the picture of a smallish, slender, freckle-faced girl in a pale green dress. Her hair, swinging around bare golden shoulders, was warm chestnut and her eyes promised something that was rich and beautiful.

"Oh," said Annie, awestruck. "It's me . . ."

David reached for her, his hands gentle

as never before. "Now perhaps we're getting somewhere, at last," he murmured wryly, and kissed her open, surprised mouth.

When she surfaced, many minutes later, Annie discovered that her mind was working overtime, reluctantly penetrating through her joy. "I don't understand—" she gasped.

David swung her legs onto the couch and grinned down at her. "Yes, you do. I've painted you because I love you. Simple isn't it?"

"You—*love* me?" A new, unbelievable world slid into her bewildered mind. It wasn't possible, of course it wasn't—and yet . . .

"I most certainly do. And you're the first woman I've ever said that to." His voice took on a new depth. "*And* the last. Now, Annie, you're not going to be difficult about this, are you, my darling?"

She saw the almost hidden anxiety behind the flash of the arrogant smile and understood. "The trouble with you is that you can't say what you really feel, David Nicholas."

"True. And only a mini-psychologist

like you could prise that admission out of me; all right, here it comes." He took a deep breath and bent his head to kiss her throat, her neck, and the shoulders that showed beneath the slipping strings of her sun-dress. "I want you to marry me, Annie—I promise I'll be loving and true, even though sometimes I'll still be selfish and . . . what was the word?"

He looked deep into her eyes and she recognised the utter truth of what he had said. He loved her, just as she loved him. It was a miracle of sorts—unlikely and astounding, but it was true. She pulled him closer to her.

"My darling, I'll marry you as soon as we can make it happen. And I'll be your friend, too, because I know that's what you need . . ." Through her bewildered joy, a sudden thought prodded and surfaced. She pushed him away and sat up. "Which reminds me—tell me about Marcus! What's going to happen about the money?"

David groaned, and thumped the couch beside her in mock desperation. "There you go! Annie, you're impossible!"

"I know I am. And that's one of the

reasons you love me—so tell me about Marcus, please, David darling . . ."

He got to his feet and wandered across the cabin, eyes never leaving hers as she sat upright, her face filled with vitality and happiness. "I'm putting up his salary; that way he can afford to repay the money he took. And I'm going to be best man at Katnina's wedding. And Alexa is all set to start running about again and will stop worrying . . ." At the window he halted, looking away down the beach, and then turning back to Annie, with a smile that intrigued her. "Come here, love. Come and look at this."

She ran across the room and with his arm about her they watched a small figure wandering alone down the sands.

"It's Alexa . . . why, she's hardly limping at all!" Annie said delightedly. David pulled her closer to him.

"Limping be damned. She's dancing!"

As they watched Alexa suddenly extended her hands and let the new-found happiness break out in a simple dance that expressed all that was within her. It was a sight Annie knew she would never forget.

She looked up at David, eyes brilliant and deeply moved.

"Talk about the happy ending to a fairy story . . . oh, I'm so glad for her . . ."

Something on his face silenced her. His arms around her strengthened and she sensed a need growing within him. He said quietly, with only a hint of the old mockery, "And now that particular story is over, do you think you could possibly allow us to write another chapter of our own story, my dear Miss Frayne?"

Sure of herself as never before, Annie took his hand and led him towards the waiting couch. "I think it would be lovely if we became joint authors from now on," she said determinedly, and pulled him down beside her.

GUIDE
TO THE COLOUR CODING
OF
ULVERSCROFT BOOKS

Many of our readers have written to us expressing their appreciation for the way in which our colour coding has assisted them in selecting the Ulverscroft books of their choice. To remind everyone of our colour coding—this is as follows:

BLACK COVERS
Mysteries

*

BLUE COVERS
Romances

*

RED COVERS
Adventure Suspense and General Fiction

*

ORANGE COVERS
Westerns

*

GREEN COVERS
Non-Fiction

ROMANCE TITLES
in the
Ulverscroft Large Print Series

The Smile of the Stranger	*Joan Aiken*
Busman's Holiday	*Lucilla Andrews*
Flowers From the Doctor	*Lucilla Andrews*
Nurse Errant	*Lucilla Andrews*
Silent Song	*Lucilla Andrews*
Merlin's Keep	*Madeleine Brent*
Tregaron's Daughter	*Madeleine Brent*
The Bend in the River	*Iris Bromige*
A Haunted Landscape	*Iris Bromige*
Laurian Vale	*Iris Bromige*
A Magic Place	*Iris Bromige*
The Quiet Hills	*Iris Bromige*
Rosevean	*Iris Bromige*
The Young Romantic	*Iris Bromige*
Lament for a Lost Lover	*Philippa Carr*
The Lion Triumphant	*Philippa Carr*
The Miracle at St. Bruno's	*Philippa Carr*
The Witch From the Sea	*Philippa Carr*
Isle of Pomegranates	*Iris Danbury*
For I Have Lived Today	*Alice Dwyer-Joyce*
The Gingerbread House	*Alice Dwyer-Joyce*
The Strolling Players	*Alice Dwyer-Joyce*
Afternoon for Lizards	*Dorothy Eden*
The Marriage Chest	*Dorothy Eden*

FICTION TITLES
in the
Ulverscroft Large Print Series

The Onedin Line: The High Seas
Cyril Abraham

The Onedin Line: The Iron Ships
Cyril Abraham

The Onedin Line: The Shipmaster
Cyril Abraham

The Onedin Line: The Trade Winds
Cyril Abraham

The Enemy	*Desmond Bagley*
Flyaway	*Desmond Bagley*
The Master Idol	*Anthony Burton*
The Navigators	*Anthony Burton*
A Place to Stand	*Anthony Burton*
The Doomsday Carrier	*Victor Canning*
The Cinder Path	*Catherine Cookson*
The Girl	*Catherine Cookson*
The Invisible Cord	*Catherine Cookson*
Life and Mary Ann	*Catherine Cookson*
Maggie Rowan	*Catherine Cookson*
Marriage and Mary Ann	*Catherine Cookson*
Mary Ann's Angels	*Catherine Cookson*
All Over the Town	*R. F. Delderfield*
Jamaica Inn	*Daphne du Maurier*
My Cousin Rachel	*Daphne du Maurier*